ON THE BRINK OF DEATH

Struggling, the two men wrestled out across a ledge—the lofty crest of Eagle Perch butte. Behind, the rimrock extended upward to form a cliff perhaps twice a score of feet in height, and hollowed out of the mass of the rock was the shallow, open-fronted area on which they fought to the death.

Demming was a big man, not as tall as Ki, but heavier. He tore his wrist from Ki's grasp and brought his revolver around to trigger point-blank. Ki ducked, using an elbow thrust to shift both Demming and himself at angles, and the revolver thundered next to his face. And then he had hold of Demming, his momentum shoving the man backwards, his left hand slashing downward in a disarming chop.

They were now at the rim. Ki found himself battling less a man than a mauling animal. He tried to swing Demming away, but the man only panicked more, grasped Ki's throat with as many fingers as he could manage, and clung for dear life, strangling Ki in the process.

Ki felt one of his feet sliding off the edge . . .

•→ WESLEY ELLIS →•

LONE STAR

AND THE
MONTANA MARAUDERS

J
JOVE BOOKS, NEW YORK

LONE STAR AND THE MONTANA MARAUDERS

A Jove Book / published by arrangement with
the author

PRINTING HISTORY
Jove edition / April 1994

ISBN: 0-515-11357-3

A JOVE BOOK®
Jove Books are published by The Berkley Publishing Group,
200 Madison Avenue, New York, New York 10016.
JOVE and the "J" design are trademarks belonging to Jove Publications, Inc.

PRINTED IN THE UNITED STATES OF AMERICA

10 9 8 7 6 5 4 3 2 1

Chapter 1

The late fall storm, promised by an angry sunrise, blew in shortly before noon. A cold breath fanned down from the northern Rockies, bearing on its wings a veil of sooty clouds. The overcast skies continued to roll lower, darker, and shortly it began to drizzle, and then to rain in wind-tossed sheets. A heavy downpour soon swept the east-central region of the Montana Territory, cascading down wooded slopes, and drenching thicket and field and the pair of riders heading north along the Billings-Saskatoon Trail.

The trail was not much at the best of times, often as not used for livestock drives. At the moment it mainly consisted of hock-deep gumbo. But it had the advantage of being the only route to wind through some 650 miles of desolate wilderness, with a number of settlements and trading posts along the way and secondary trails angling off to places such as Roundup; Lewistown; Malta; Port of Morgan, on the border; and Swift Current, across in Canada. The two riders were not going all that distance; their plans were to stop about 90 miles above Billings, in the hellfire town of Spots.

They rode slumped, weary, soaked, and chilled to the bone by the rainstorm, although both Jessica Starbuck and Ki wore tan mackinaws and broad-brimmed hats. Jessie did not appear to be what she really was—a proud, aristocratic woman in her mid-twenties; a crack shot with her holstered revolver and the twin-shot derringer concealed behind her belt buckle; and a shrewd, knowledgeable heiress to immense wealth, the Starbuck international business empire. Her long coppery-blond hair was tucked up under the crown of her sodden brown Stetson, and though the mackinaw covered her flannel shirt, denim jacket, and much of her jeans, it failed to conceal the firm thrust of her breasts or the sensual curves of her thighs and buttocks. And despite an expression mirroring the exhausting effects of her journey, the warmth of Jessie's sultry face, with its high cheekbones, audacious green eyes, and the provocative if challenging quirk of her lips, could not be dampened by the autumnal storm.

Similarly, Ki seemed to be little more than a tall, lean man in his early thirties, of mixed Japanese and Caucasian blood, and so peaceful by nature that he lacked a gun belt or any other sign of a firearm. In fact, he was a samurai-trained master of martial arts, in whose old leather vest were secreted short daggers and similar small throwing weapons, including razor-edged star-shaped steel disks called *shuriken*. Upon immigrating to America, Ki had been hired by Jessie's father, Alex Starbuck, to protect his daughter. Consequently, Ki and Jessie had virtually grown up together, and after her father's murder it seemed only fitting for him to stay on, but as loyal confidant to the young heiress. She took control of her huge inheritance and far-flung responsibilities, proving to be strong and capable and harder than a keg of railroad spikes when need be. As close as any blood brother and sister, working together, they made a formidable team.

Before long the downpour lost its frigid sting and gradually tapered off as the storm rolled on southward. Jessie and Ki relaxed, conversing in low tones and soothing their skittish, tuckered mounts. They'd ridden steadily from Billings, where they'd been attending the annual fall horse races, until an urgent plea for help from Flora Hullinger, granddaughter of Spots' sheriff, had cut their brief vacation short. They'd had to buy horses and gear, since Billings liveries insisted rental nags be returned within a week. Fortunately, they'd found Jessie a tough, sure-footed sorrel mare, and Ki had picked a moro gelding that had sand and bottom to spare.

Now they rode the stone ledges and rough brakes, able to maintain a slow but steady pace until abruptly the muddy trail veered in along the rim of a gorge. The gorge was steeply sloped, hopper-shaped, heavily overgrown with pine and scrub, with the bed of a rain-swollen rapids-strewn river serving as its floor.

"The North Willow," Jessie surmised, gazing down at the river.

"Well, that means it won't be long until we reach Spots," Ki said, "assuming we can cross over without drowning ourselves."

Eventually the trail led down to a ford, where the bank dipped in a rounded, swaybacked slope. Here the river was slightly wider, appearing to swirl in gentler swells between the base of a long series of cascades and the beginning angle of a sharp curve. Nonetheless, the ford was a treacherous crossing. Even here the river was bedded with fanged rocks, and the far bank was a tall bluff gashed with numerous side gullies.

It was small wonder that they should eye it with scant favor. Their disapproval was not lessened by the sight of a two-horse, canopy-top Handy wagon securely wedged in the mud where the trail reached the water's edge below. A man was aimlessly sloshing about the embedded wheels. On the high driver's seat perched a slim figure garbed in a blue brocade dress, with chestnut curls peeking out from under a floppy-brimmed hat.

"Looks like a girl holding the reins," Ki mused.

"Ah Lord! If there's a young woman within a thousand miles, you'll manage to bump across her," Jessie huffed. "Leave her be."

"But they're stuck. It's only polite to help."

Soon they pulled up beside the stalled wagon. The man, wearing bib overalls and a linsey-woolsey shirt, was quite elderly, scratching his white hair while squinting up at them. The girl was no more than twenty, probably less; she gave them a questioning glance from a pair of very big, very auburn, and very long-lashed eyes. She had a tip-tilted little straight nose, the bridge of which was powdered by a few freckles. Her cheeks were creamily tanned, her mouth very red, the lips soft and sweetly curved. When Ki smiled at her, she smiled back instinctively, showing a dimple at one corner of her red mouth.

Jessie regarded the old man. "Need some help?"

"Sure do," he croaked. "Don't rightly reckon what you can do, though. I'd hazard we're here to stay if I can't wrangle an extra team or two up in town."

Now Ki turned his attention to the wagon. His gaze centered first on the barrels, boxes, and other cargo piled in the bed behind the seat; and then on the long, wide, and heavy boards that were lashed to either side to facilitate floating the wagon across the swollen river.

4

"I've an idea," he said after a thoughtful moment, "that if we unload the stuff in the back of your wagon and shove those planks under the front wheels, your team plus our horses might be able to pull the wagon free."

"But how're you going to get the planks under the wheels?"

"Suppose we unhitch 'em and make a try to figure it," Ki answered, dismounting near the man.

The girl, looking down from her perch, smiled demurely. "Hadn't I better get down? That'll make the load lighter."

Ki ran his glance over her slender form. "Not much more'n a hundred pounds," he calculated. "Reckon that won't make much difference one way or the other. No sense in getting your feet wet, ma'am."

Jessie, ankle-high in mud, rolled her eyes.

The girl had the grit to step down anyway, and pitch in, never minding how muddy she got her dress or shoes. The four of them soon had the cargo unloaded and stacked on a little rise of ground near the wagon. Then they freed the boards. Ki took one and shoved the end against the wheel where it sank into the sticky mud, then cupped his hands under the hub. "Okay, now when I lift the wheel, you push the plank under. All set?"

The old man stared at him. "Son, you look sorta husky, but you can't lift that wheel. You're talkin' loco."

"Maybe so, but you just get ready to shove."

Backing up to the wheel, Ki bent his knees and grasped two spokes in his hands. The wagon creaked, groaned, and rocked as the wheel rose slowly from the mud. "Quick, shove 'er under," he ordered through clenched teeth.

Sputtering amazement, the old man obeyed.

Ki eased the wheel down upon the heavy oak support.

"Now the other one," he said, catching his breath as he moved around to the far side of the wagon.

Another moment of intense effort and the chore was done. The old man gaped at Ki. "If I hadn't seed it, I never would've believed it!"

"A dumb steer is a lot stronger," Ki responded, grinning. "Now wait till we swing loops on the pole and tie in our horses. Then whoop to your team, and with a little luck we'll have your wagon out no worse for wear."

A few minutes later the old man let out a bellow. The girl called out as well, flicking a whip at the team. At the same time Jessie and Ki goaded their straining horses forward. The taut ropes hummed like harp strings. The front wagon wheels ground solidly against their oaken supports and began to turn. The wagon lurched, then rumbled up out of the mud bog and came to a halt on a patch of loose shale and gravel, just a few feet from the water's edge.

Ki, dismounting, strode to the pole and unlooped his and Jessie's ropes—then straightened abruptly, turning with Jessie toward the sound of approaching horses. Three riders appeared at the crest of the bluff on the opposite bank, galloped down the trail, and splashed without hesitation into the river. Its swift current rose almost horse-belly high, but the men waded recklessly ahead, busy with spur. Staring at the oncoming trio, the girl in the wagon gave a gasp, and the old man cussed disgustedly under his breath.

The riders swept up onto the bank and reined in a score of paces from the wagon. Foremost was a big burly man with a bearded face and a truculent eye, his brows drawn together in a scowl. His voice rang out, harsh, peremptory. "Yuh was warned to get out and

6

not come back, yuh ol' fart. An' you two there, yuh get the same warnin'. We don't hanker for strangers in this section!"

Ki sauntered toward the man, smiling blandly. "That so?"

"Yeah, that's so!"

"Too bad," Ki replied mildly, "'cause folks sometimes get what they don't hanker for."

The man's heavy face darkened. His hard mouth set like a rattrap. Ki moseyed closer, eyeing all three men carefully. They wore ordinary range garb in sad need of washing, caked cowboots, and holstered revolvers, and they had a certain hardcase stamp to them, tight of mouth and long on twist.

The man growled down at Ki, "You and your female, you mount up and turn around pronto and hit the trail back south."

"Our horses always go the way they're headed," Ki replied. "And right now they're headed for Spots."

The big rider's jaw dropped slightly; he shifted in his saddle, his right hand stabbing for his revolver.

Leaping, Ki grabbed the man by the shirt and hauled him loose of the saddle. Down 'n' dirty came the man, losing his pistol and diving like a cannonball, ramming full-bodied into Ki. The force knocked Ki backward off his feet, with the man falling atop him and flailing him with both fists.

The other two men barked protests, fumbling for their revolvers. Jessie beat them to the draw. "Stop it, boys, or I'll stop you with lead!"

Ki and the man rolled over and over in the mud, hammering at each other. Ki was ready to maim him, but held off using his martial arts, feeling wringy enough to humiliate the man in front of his own men, whipping

7

him at his own game, the down 'n' dirty gutter brawl. A slanting blow to the man's left eyebrow drew blood. The man jabbed a thumb at Ki's eyeball, only to take a knuckle in the throat that set him to gagging, his hands dropping. Immediately Ki shoved free and launched to his feet.

Scrambling, the man rushed in with arms swinging like windmills. Ki dodged a high left, weaved in close, and buried a stiff jab in the man's midriff. The man gasped and bent, still swinging, and received a split second left-right combo to both eyes. Then the man scored an uppercutting haymaker that crunched against Ki's jaw with meaty impact, sending him staggering off balance. Shaking his head to clear it, Ki glimpsed Jessie holding her pistol centered implacably on the two pals, though that didn't squelch the man from demanding gun action from them.

"You got irons! No female pistol-packer's any lady or any shootist!"

"That's what we're afeared of," one man replied. "She might go wavery and hit us if she takes a notion to fire point-blank!"

Blurting an oath, the man charged Ki to polish him off. Ki evaded the storming fists, dancing aside and hammering at the man's gut and heart. The counter caught the man surprised and unguarded, and though he tried to slug back, Ki kept darting around and under, pummeling the belly and face, driving the man down to the water's edge. Rebounding, grappling, the man tried to wrap Ki in a crushing bear hug. Suspecting such a move, Ki was prepared for it and caught the man by the whiskers, jerking his face down, mashing the nose against his rising right knee. He felt the cartilage crush, saw the blood from the flattened nostrils as he pushed the man aside. Like a blundering blind bull, the man shuffled and charged head down, groping, ignoring Ki's hits, battering through Ki's guard, and taking a jab on the top of the head that almost cracked Ki's knuckles. Then the man got his arms around Ki, lifted him, whirled and heaved him away.

Ki struck the sodden earth with a bone-shaking splash.

"Will yuh quit stallin'?" the man roared at his pals. "I'd shoot him m'self, but my gun's full of mud now. F'Gawd's sake, pull your drop on him!"

"Pull, and you'll push grass," Jessie warned.

The man's mouth clamped, and his eyes were ebony fire. "By hell!"

But the other two sat still, continuing to respect Jessie's pistol more than the big man's honor. Bellowing, the man loped at Ki, blood trickling from his nose and mouth, one eye closed, and the other puffed and bruised. Yet the homicidal light burned from his injured face as his sharp-heeled boot canted toward Ki's chest. Desperately Ki wrenched aside, grasping the man's descending foot to avert the crippling stomp. But he was not quite fast enough. The boot tramped down upon his left shoulder. Hot lances of agony ripped through his bludgeoned sinews. With his hand still clasped around the boot, he coiled his legs beneath the man's belly and thrust upward with all his strength. Retching, the man reeled back toppling askew and fell flat on his face.

Ki pounced on the man before he could recover. Snatching a fistful of his shaggy hair, Ki pounded his head up and down with a wicked, rhythmical beat, grinding and drumming the man senseless. Then, wavering, Ki rose and glared down, panting, at the man lying half submerged and unmoving in the mire.

"He's all yours," he said to the glum-faced pair as he

9

dragged the man by the collar to his horse. He lifted the man and dumped him unceremoniously into his saddle.

The man groped for his saddle horn to keep from falling, cursing luridly—mainly at his pals. "Y'all 'er pissants!" he spat through bloodied lips, slumped over and wavering. "One bullet would've done it."

"Take him back to whatever coyote hole you all crawled out of," Jessie snapped angrily. *"Now!"*

As the three riders splashed back across the river Jessie holstered her pistol and drew a Winchester .44-40 from her saddle boot. The departing horsemen, glancing back over their shoulders, could see the carbine ready for business. One shook a furious hand. Then they all faced front and sent their horses surging up the trail. In another moment they bulged over the crest of the bluff and were gone from sight.

The old man cackled. "Son, m' name's Greene, mostly knowed hereabouts as Red Greene. And this's my niece, Violet. Put 'er there." He glanced questioningly as he extended a gnarled paw.

Shaking hands, Ki introduced himself and Jessie, then remarked, "I gather you live around here?"

"T'uther side of Spots, to the nor'west a tad," Red Greene answered. "Own the Rocking-G spread, an' I tell you here 'n now I could use a top hand about your size. Got a couple of waddies ridin' for me what was born the year after Noah landed the Ark, an' I'm plumb willin' to pay right, for the right man."

"Notion I could do worse. I'll think it over," Ki said with a sidelong grin at Jessie. "We want to have a look around Spots first, though."

"Wal, okay," Greene said, and glanced up at the girl on the seat. "Violet, take a gander at this feller so you can tell folks that for once in your life you seed a man!"

"Uncle Red! You talk too much," his niece rebuked tartly, reddening from embarrassment and annoyance. Her piquant face mirrored concern, however, as she gazed toward where the unsavory trio had vanished across the river. Red Greene followed her glance, and his own face grew grave.

"She's scairt you made some bad enemies today, son," he said.

Jessie responded, "Those three? Who are they?"

"Wal, ma'am, I don't rightly know their names, only that they're killers. Twice over killers, to be per'xact. Fust it was Loren Estleman, of the Square-E. His carcass was found swingin' from a tree seven, eight miles up beyond Spots. Then John Lutz, another ranch owner, was back-shot mysterious-like."

"How do you know the ranchers were murdered by those men?"

"By them, or gun-flunkies like 'em. Y'see, Miz Starbuck, their victims are always warned ahead of time," Greene explained. "Estleman and Lutz both reported receivin' notes warnin' 'em to get out or die but just figured some cowpokes were tryin' to booger 'em."

"And you?"

Greene seemed to squirm a bit. "Yeah, I hafta admit I got a warnin', too. Me, I didn't pay no attention to it any more'n they did—till now. Now you know as much as any of us do, I'm afeard."

Red Greene would have been stunned to have learned that Jessie already knew as much as he, and probably more. At that very moment there reposed in a pocket of her shirt a note—printed on a piece of pulp paper, the kind of cheap stock that newspapers are printed on—that had been sent to Sheriff Ichabod Hullinger,

11

warning him to leave Spots or face deadly vengeance. For some time Starbuck field representatives in Montana had been sending dispatches to her company headquarters at Jessie's Circle Star ranch in Texas, relating incidents of Crow, Sioux, and other Indians attacking settlers, ranchers, hunters, and transportation routes. Then the previous August, Fort Maginnis had been established forty miles northeast of Lewistown to serve as a base of supply and operations against the hostile Indians. But lately, as the Indian threat had been diminishing new dangers had been growing. Ranchers in this region were facing ruin through wholesale rustlings and raidings, and even facing death. Some of them had cattle spreads, but most ran small horse outfits and had been hoping to cash in on Fort Maginnis' urgent need for military mounts. In fact, in order to supply the fort, horse ranchers from Sheridan and points farther south had been pooling their stock and herding them north along this trail; recently these ranchers had been complaining that their trail bosses were reporting their remudas of horses stolen en route, with most of the horse thievery centering around Spots.

Although keeping track of these depredations, Jessie had not taken action because Starbuck interests had not been directly affected. Then Flora Hullinger had appealed for help, enclosing the warning note that her grandfather had received and begging Jessie to dispatch a large number of men to the beleaguered town to bring the mysterious killers to bay. Flora's desperate plea had been sufficient for Jessie to immediately head for Spots. A decade before, Ichabod Hullinger had sided Jessie's father against a gang of outlaws at great personal risk, without question or compensation. Alex Starbuck had never been able to repay the sheriff's courage, his every offer to help being politely but firmly declined. Even after his wife, son, and daughter-in-law had been massacred by Sioux, Hullinger had refused to be "beholden." But Alex Starbuck never forgot a debt or a friend; neither did Jessie. After ten years Ichabod Hullinger needed help, and help he would get. With interest . . .

"Actually, Miz Starbuck," Red Greene continued, "the best advice I can give you an' Ki is to turn your horses 'round and head right back the way you come."

"Thanks," Jessie replied quietly. "I'm not taking it."

"Didn't reckon you would," Greene said with a sigh. "Wal, let's get going. We're heading home with a load of supplies from Billings, and the long haul has plumb tuckered out these ol' bones of mine."

As soon as the planks were reattached to the wagon, Red Greene took his seat next to Violet, picked up the reins, and hurrawed his team forward. On either side of the wagon Jessie and Ki urged their mounts to water's edge, the horses prancing, shying. Jessie kept firm rein and kneed her sorrel mare until, reluctantly, it plunged up to its hocks into the river. Urged on by Ki, his moro gelding struggled across, hoofs fighting for purchase on the slippery, sharp rocks, legs resisting the buffeting of the churning current.

They were midway across when the first rifle shot sounded.

★

Chapter 2

Red Greene's hat flew off as if smitten by some great and invisible hand, and smack-dab through its brim was drilled the burning tunnel of a big-bore slug. He ducked low, unscathed but unnerved; Ki lunged in his saddle to help him; Violet screamed; and the bullet, ricocheting off a metal seat bracket, angled up through the front panel and slashed a bloody furrow along the broad rump of one of the wagon team. The piercing whinnies of first one, then both, rearing, plunging horses and the rumbling shift of cargo as the wagon swayed to and fro added to the noisy bedlam. The frenzied animals bolted headlong into the current, Red Greene fighting a set of taut reins that wrenched and jerked like angry snakes in his hands.

The wagon caromed off a large boulder, and Greene tried to avoid the next one by reining sharply. His panicked team responded to his frantic pull by whirling completely about, ramming into each other and crashing against the boulder. The wild swerve had tilted the wagon dangerously, and Greene fought to balance it with his weight; but the cargo in back toppled sideward, shoving

15

the wagon beyond its center of gravity.

"Jump!" he yelled. "Jump!" Greene released the reins and dived off, Violet a kick behind him, and then the wagon was tipping over, rolling entirely over and almost drowning the floundering team.

Meanwhile, Jessie and Ki were desperately trying to keep their own horses from bolting. They were unable to help Red Greene as he lunged for a hold on the side of the overturned wagon just as another blast of lead ripped into the water alongside. Violet, careening against the wagon, struck open water on the downstream side and plunged under the surface.

Without a breath of delay, Ki leaped from the saddle and dived after her, ignoring the bullet that whined past his head. Dazed and gasping, Violet surfaced, only to be caught by the surging current. Ki swam furiously in an effort to intercept her. He reached out, missed, stroked, and reached again, fingers tightening on the collar of her dress. Then he battled for the north bank, trying to resist the tide that was inexorably sweeping them toward boulders through which the river was cascading in deadly foaming rapids.

"Violet!" Red Greene yelled as he glimpsed her and Ki rolling momentarily on the crest of a wave and then they disappeared. "Hang on, gal! Hang on! I'm comin'!"

"No!" Jessie called before he let go of the wagon. "They've gone too far for us to be able to help in time. Ki's a good swimmer, and he's the only one who's got a chance to save her. Quick now—let go and head for shore!"

"I, ah, I can't swim," Greene confessed.

"Great. And you were going to save your niece," Jessie muttered under her breath, and hastily grabbing the coiled lariat from the pommel of her saddle, she tossed Greene one end. "Tie it to the sideboard there!"

"But . . ." Distraught and confused, Greene muttered as he snatched up the line and knotted it firmly to where he was holding onto the wagon. Simultaneously, Jessie wound the other end of the rope to her saddle horn, and then urged her frantic horse shoreward. She heard the slap of lead hitting the river water and wished she could have headed for the south shore instead, but the south was the side on which a churning, tearing jumble of boulders and cascades began wedging out across the river, leaving her no choice but to go right toward the rifle fire targeting them from the bluff.

The frantic team was wrestling against the tangle of harness caused by the overturning of the wagon, but the two horses tried gallantly to follow Jessie's lead, the lure of dry land apparently appealing to them as well. Jessie angled diagonally for a spot on the shore that had a concealing thicket of brush and saplings, glimpsing the wagon wallowing some yards behind and tangential to her. Her sorrel fought for a hold on the hard, slick surface of the north bank, wading the last few feet. Exhausted and stumbling for balance, the horse climbed out of the water. Dismounting, Jessie freed the slip-knotted lariat from her saddle and tied it around a granite boulder.

The lariat snapped taut, and for an instant it seemed impossible that it could hold the pull of the wagon. The current was strong and fought hard to hold its impetuous grip, yet now its force acted in their favor. The wagon yanked around in a dizzy arc, then reeled joltingly as it grounded on the brush-covered bank, its team scrambling for footing, huffing and shivering for a recuperative moment.

"We're stuck solid!" Greene panted, his voice

17

trembling with relief as he stumbled from the wagon up the bank. "Now to find Violet—"

They were found instead by bullets. From the stony bluff above, the rifle sent lead stitching around Greene and Jessie.

"Get to cover!" Jessie shouted.

They scrambled for the sheltering brush as orange flashes and cracks of gunpowder burst from the cliff. Slugs hit the wagon. Earthen grit and rock shards flew into Jessie's face. She hunkered with Greene in the first low-cropped fringe of boulders and bush, pinned down. Her firearms were water soaked, and their only other weapon was a bowie knife she had glimpsed sheathed at Greene's belt. She was gratified that so far she and Greene had miraculously escaped harm, but she knew that any second one or both of them could expect to be hit.

She turned to Greene. "Lend me your knife."

Courteously he obliged, asking, "Wha' fo'?"

"What for! We've got to take that ambusher out, that's what for."

"You?" Greene was genuinely appalled. "You're mad."

"Mad enough to want to stay alive—which neither of us will be soon at this rate. You keep down, out of sight," she ordered in a tone brooking no argument. She began crawling toward the cliff, ignoring Greene's spluttering protests behind her.

During the frantic moments while Jessie and Greene were struggling to salvage the wagon along with their lives Ki had been helping Violet fight out of the river as the tugging current swept them through rapids and around a sharp bend.

18

"Hang onto me!" he called.

Immediately, unquestioningly, she obeyed. She clasped her arms around his neck from behind, and he moved ahead with a powerful stroke. It seemed like agonizing hours, but finally his rope-soled slippers scraped against stone, and Ki half climbed, half crawled into a shallow break. The backwash of this break in the bank created a swirling eddy, and two or three strokes took them to the river's edge, where, by clutching at an overhanging limb of a spruce, Ki was able at last to haul them both out of the cold rushing water.

He half dragged Violet across to a patch of grass. She was laughing deliriously, and did not appear to be hurt. "You saved me!" she panted, and then she laughed again.

"But not your uncle or Jessie," Ki said, grimly listening to the sporadic exchange of gunfire. "C'mon, we've got to go back."

"No!" She grabbed his arm. "Sit down. Rest."

"No time for that!"

"Don't leave me alone! Please, just a second. I'm pooped." She pulled Ki down beside her, and it was then he noticed that her exertions had worked open the upper buttons of her dress, exposing her firm, perky breasts to view. "Anyway, Ki, I want to thank you." She kissed him, then, and nibbled his ear, cooing, "I'd never have made it myself, and this is how I want to thank you."

"Fine. Now you've thanked me."

"Not enough." And she kissed him again, harder. Violet was young—not too young, but young enough—and time was pressing, but it was difficult to resist temptation.

Ki kissed her in return, his lips laving down her neck.

"No, no . . ." she mewed, wriggling without drawing away.

Then he moved to her breasts, which had been exposed so tantalizingly.

"Oh, that tickles," she gasped. "Stop, oh . . . stop . . ."

Ki stopped, chuckling. "So much for thanking me. Now up and at 'em, girl. I'm insisting. Your uncle and Jessie are under fire."

"You're right," she admitted, scrambling to her feet. "But I really was awfully winded. Oh, if anything's happened to Uncle Red . . ."

Ki took her by the hand and began propelling her quickly along the bank. "If something has, you won't be alone," he consoled. "You've still got your parents and p'raps other relatives to—"

"Parents!" she exclaimed in a deprecating tone. "My mother was a . . . a dancehall girl. She died of consumption, and as for my father, well, I don't know who he was for sure, though I understand he was a travelin' salesman in ladies' finery. Uncle Red's been the only family I've ever known or loved. Say, I still hurt from that tumblin' about I took. Can't you slow down?"

Ki shook his head and continued forging swiftly through the trees and bushes that bordered the bend in the river, their pace helping the afternoon sun, such as it was, to dry their clothing. Veering, they thrust through some entangling foliage and poised on the bank—craning for a clear view and fearing for the worst, for they had not heard any shots for some moments now.

Squeezing close beside Ki, Violet pointed upriver, then smiled. "Look, they've got the wagon 'n' team on the bank. They must be safe under cover in those rocks and trees there, where the shooter can't get at them."

Ki nodded. "Well, the rifleman's quit for now, anyway."

"We don't have to hurry so fast, Ki."

"But they'll be worried about us, and we—"

"The tumble I got," she cut in, groaning and soulfully wincing. "I bet I've got a big bruise." She stepped back a pace, just enough to conceal herself in the overhanging copse and give her room to gather her damp dress and lift it to her waist. She turned and pouted over her shoulder at Ki. "Do you see anything?"

"Nothing," Ki said, and in a sense it was true, for Violet was not wearing pantaloons, bloomers, a corset, or anything else under her dress. What Ki saw was that she was buck naked, her plump bottom showing rosy and dappled in the filtered daylight. He became aroused, but he was also growing weary of her flirting and wondered how far she'd go before turning off again. In any case, the quickest cure seemed to be a dose like before, so he stepped close, slid an arm around her, and kissed her. She reacted with enthusiasm, the pressure of her body like an eager promise, her mouth gluing to his, eyes closed, nostrils quivering, her curious hand sliding to his waist.

So that was her game! Her earlier denials were just for the record, in case anyone should accuse her of being too easy. Ki broke the kiss, but before he could say anything, her fingers were moving to find the bulge at his groin and travel its length. Deftly, then, she untied his rope belt and popped the top button. She lifted her mouth from his and twisted slightly, Ki sensing she was hot with anticipation as she unbuttoned his fly and tugged his jeans down. He arched his hips, and she used both hands to grasp and begin to massage the exposed shaft of his erection.

"You said we're in a hurry, so hurry," she whispered throatily, "but not on the ground, with all this mud and runoff."

"Not going to take this lying down, eh?" Ki positioned his crotch against her while she wriggled in an odd mixture of trepidation and desire, gingerly reaching between her legs to aim him toward her pink cleft. Flesh met flesh, seeking that rapturous lodging, the hard within the soft. As the experienced martial artist conquered by seeming to yield, so the female conquered by accepting the thrust.

"God, you feel good," she sighed as he slid, rigid and thick, deep inside her. She was small, tight, and Ki felt compressed by moist softness, surrounded by slick heat. He began to pump.

"This's insane," she panted, pistoning against him. "But I tell you, Ki, if I don't get my itch scratched once a week, I simply fall to pieces. And what with Uncle Red's taking us to Billings to shop and back, the week's way overdue."

"You mean you schedule this?"

"Sexing should never be haphazard. That'd be like animals."

Thrusting harder, Ki was unwilling to argue. Violet moaned deliriously, half standing, half crouching as she ground against him in a harsh, quick union of needy desire. Ki hammered into her wanton depths while she gasped and humped in concert, lost in lust, with her devouring frenzy stimulating Ki to a savage tempo. She undulated her thighs in a mania of passion, heaving her womanhood back and against him and then, to make it more fulfilling, reaching a hand to massage his scrotum gently.

Her rhythm increased as her orgasm approached. It

22

was Ki, however, who climaxed first. He released so fast, so furiously, that he was almost chagrined—until he realized that she, too, was pounding and squeezing inner muscles in time with his pulsatings. Soft muscles moved in spasms of delight, enclosing him tightly, throbbing ecstatically. She bent her legs wider, pushing back with pelvic force, trapping the final sparks of pleasure.

"You like?" She giggled a happy, rippling sound of joy.

"I like," Ki sighed, withdrawing.

Violet straightened, letting her dress fall and primly smoothing out its wrinkles with her hand. "There's more next week—"

Her invitation was shattered by the sudden, savage bark of rifle fire. Ki, hitching his jeans, sprang to the bank.

"They're in trouble again!" he snapped. "C'mon, Violet, let's go!"

She needed no urging. She raced after Ki as he sprinted upriver through the dense underbrush.

Jessie by now had wormed through the bank's weedy scrub and boulders to the base of the cliff, where she crouched motionless for a moment as she considered her next move. Thicker brush covered the slope roughly halfway, and from there on stretched a rising jumble of stony outcrops and stands of pine. Against the bushwhacker she had only Greene's hunting knife, yet she was determined to stop him from slaying and fleeing. She hoped she could capture him alive to answer her questions, but if it came down to kill or be killed, so be it.

First, though, she had to get him.

Hunching low, Jessie worked her way up the sloping

bank in a circuitous route, wishing to hurry and yet knowing her only prayer lay in avoiding detection. She didn't hesitate at the top fringe of the brush, but plunged on up into the pines, their resinous scent heavy about her. She avoided crossing gravel and loose shale as much as possible, taking advantage of bare ledges and troughlike depressions, parting scraggly undergrowth carefully and slipping through with hardly a sound. Gradually, implacably shifting higher, she reached a stratum of wind-stunted lodgepole pine growing near the rim of the crest. She paused, glancing briefly through the slight opening in the limbs at the lowering sun, aware of the silence that had dropped with startling abruptness. The faint, sad ripple of water in the river below was the only sound.

Bending her head, tuning her senses to their peak sensitivity, she waited, breathing softly . . . until at last she heard a telltale noise, the soft-spitted slap of an ejected stream of tobacco juice.

Between Jessie and that chaw of tobacco was a sharp slope, followed by more brush and rock. The stone face of the slope was as slippery as grease, and the slope angled so steeply that Jessie had to slither on elbows and knees until she could wedge into the scrub. Ahead loomed a great huddle of conical stones flanking an outward-jutting spur of the cliff. Hidden movement on their far side was barely discernible, but it was enough for her to zero in on as she snaked through the brushy growth and slid between the tall cracked rocks.

Ki had trained Jessie well. Using his techniques, she bellied in quietly from the left and saw the shadowy outline of a big man lying prone in the spur's clearing. The clearing was V-shaped, the spur, like the prow of a ship, thrusting out and overlooking the ford in the river and protected on both sides by low-slabbed boulders. Across from Jessie the broad rear of the clearing continued on around the hill to where, she supposed, some sort of path connected it to the trail below. Up at the apex of the clearing, where there was no stone, the gunman was stretched out and sighting down at the riverbank, shouldering a Spencer .56-50 Indian model repeater. There was no mistaking the figure; it was the bruiser Ki had beaten back at the ford. Where his pals were Jessie had no idea, but because up till now there had only been one rifleman shooting down at the wagon, she doubted the two others were siding him here and now. Like as not, she reckoned, he had returned on a private mission of vengeance while they had gone on to report to whoever had sent them. And she very much wanted to know just who that "whoever" was.

Problem was, the clearing was layered with pebbly gravel, the kind that crunches underfoot no matter how softly one treads. Jessie was not close enough to launch an unarmed attack, and she seriously doubted she could sneak close enough and still catch the man off guard— and she knew from experience that while knives have many superior qualities, outmaneuvering a point-blank bullet wasn't one of them. She'd have to bluff the man into surrender.

Jessie rose from the rocks, fingering the knife. "Not a sound, not a move, you're surrounded," she snapped coldly, walking noisily in her boots. "Give one peep, one twitch, and we'll blow you to smithereens."

The man, flat with his back more or less to Jessie, didn't say a word, but he sure moved. Like a scalded ferret he moved, swiveling about and firing as rapidly as he could, displaying some of the quickest reflexes Jessie had ever witnessed.

Ironically, he was too swift. He triggered a split-second too soon in his swing and missed, while twisting too fast for Jessie to aim a wounding blow accurately. Before the man could squeeze off a properly lined shot, the hunting knife speared, slicing deep into his partially exposed chest. The man rolled wailing, the rifle blasting, blasting a second time harmlessly into the air, and blood spewed out like steam out of a geyser.

The wide blade had inadvertently severed a main artery. Jessie ran to the man, cursing her luck. The man just seemed to deflate before her eyes, his life draining out in pumping spurts, then dribbles, then nothing, the ground beneath him becoming a thirsty crimson muck. The man died exceedingly quickly.

Moving the rifle aside, Jessie dragged the body to a dry patch and searched his pockets, discovering nothing of significance. The dead ambusher remained a stranger.

Rising, Jessie angled to the far rear of the clearing and went around the side of the hill. There, as she'd supposed, was a narrow, little-used path that dipped winding along the hillside in the direction of the trail. There was a horse ground-reined by the path, placidly grazing; she recognized the mount as the one the man had been riding down at the ford, but checking it over now, she found only that it bore a meaningless brand, and its loose-cinched rig was regulation rangeland gear, with no outstanding peculiarities.

Jessie mounted the horse and began riding down the path, figuring to hit the trail and then head down along the bank to the thicket where she'd left Red Greene. Instead, to her vast relief and delight, she ran across Greene, Ki, and Violet, hiking as fast as they could to meet her. They stopped to exchange short accounts of their travails.

"Our next step is to righten the wagon and continue on to Spots," Red Greene declared as they all began down to the river again. "I can't thank you enough, Miz Starbuck. And you, too, Ki. Y'all have saved us both."

Violet nodded, smiling brightly. "And please come visit us at our ranch. Next week at this time, f'sure."

"Why next week at this time?" Jessie asked, puzzled.

Ki cleared his throat. "Forget it. Just a notion."

"Uh-huh, just a little something straight we got between us," Violet added, giggling. "It's not important. Easy come, easy go."

"Stifle your joshing, gal," Greene told his niece with perplexed annoyance.

Jessie glanced at Violet and then at Ki. And when they were almost back to the wagon, she maneuvered Ki aside and told him in a low whisper, "You ought to be ashamed of yourself!"

"What?"

"I don't know how you do it. And with such a sweet young thing."

"Violet? Now, wait a min—"

"It's scandalous. You must've caught her from behind, Ki. That's the only explanation. You got her when her back was turned. . . ."

★

Chapter 3

After salvaging as much of the cargo as practical, Jessie, Ki, and the Greenes set off for nearby Spots, keeping a wary eye out for further trouble. Fortunately, the rest of the trip passed uneventfully, and they reached the small town around the dinner hour. There, at the livery stable, they parted company, the Greenes heading homeward while Jessie and Ki turned their mounts over to the hostler for tending.

As they were leaving the livery Jessie asked the hostler, "By the way, where did the name of the town come from? Was there a Mr. Spots who founded it?"

"Naw," the rheumy-eyed oldster answered. "It come by its name naturallike. Y'know how in the winter everyone advises you, 'Watch out when you're ridin', it's icy in spots'? And how during spring and fall rains they're always advisin', 'Watch out, it's bog-muddy in spots'? Wal, this's the spots. Don't worry about your cayuses, folks. They'll be ready whenever you is."

"That's nice to know. There's been a rash of horse thieving around here, I understand."

"But not *here*, ma'am. Not at my stable. Only once

since I set up business did a coupla jiggers try to lift a horse."

"That right?" Ki replied. "What'd they do?"

The hostler glanced meaningfully at a sawed-off shotgun hanging on a hook at the foot of the haymow stairs. "Died!"

Hefting their traveling bags, Ki walked with Jessie to the town's only hotel. Masquerading behind the high-sounding title of the Ritz Palace, the hotel was a rambling two-story clapboard structure sharing a block of the main street with what appeared to be a long abandoned theater whose faded false front acclaimed it as the Spots Grand National Opera House. Other than these, and a courthouse with an ugly square clock tower, the town's buildings consisted of single-story shops with porch awnings, unpainted wooden barns with tar-paper roofs, and a pair of dancehall saloons facing each other across a block-square plaza. Befitting the town, the majority of pedestrians and riders were ranchhands, drovers, and teamsters passing through, but there was a sprinkling of tight-lipped, watchful men who kept largely to themselves and whose hands bore no marks of hard labor, though in garb and bearing there was little to differentiate them from the others.

After checking in at the hotel, Jessie and Ki went to the sheriff's office, which was sandwiched between a mercantile and a locksmith's shop. Entering, they found two men playing checkers at a table. One was short, paunchy, his moon face scowling in concentration as he sat, one elbow on the table, studying the checkerboard. The other man was leaning back, obviously pleased at having left his opponent in some predicament; he was ruggedly built, crowding forty, with a leonine mane of iron-gray hair and cheeks like ripe pippins. And when

30

he glanced up at the entrance of Jessie and Ki, they saw by his blank expression and dark glasses that the man was blind.

"We're looking for Sheriff Hullinger," Jessie said.

"You're lookin' at Hullinger's deputy, ma'am, Gresham Winters," the blind man said, gesturing across the board at the moon-faced man. "You come a mite too late to see Ike Hullinger, I reckon."

Jessie felt a chill. "He's not hurt, is he?"

"No, he's off having supper," Deputy Winters answered, turning from the board to eye them with a quizzical expression. "And just who d'you happen to be?"

They exchanged introductions, Jessie and Ki learning in the process that the blind man's name was Thurlow Bunce and that he was the locksmith whose shop was next door to the sheriff's office. After Jessie explained that they were old family friends of Hullinger and his granddaughter, Deputy Winters grinned and stood up, almost upsetting the checkerboard.

"Wal, Miz Starbuck, what say I show you the way over to Sheriff Ike's place. He'll be mighty pleased to have a friendly visit, what with all the travails an' woes we've been experiencin' recently." As they left the office and started along the boardwalk Winters linked his hand through the blind locksmith's arm and went on to say, "Ma'am, on second thought, p'raps you shouldn't have come. We've had a bad time, sufferin' wide-loopin's an' raidin's an' killin's, and drovers and ranchers are losin' their tempers, fightin' and feudin' around town. Ain't that right, Thurlow?"

"Maybe so, but we shouldn't scare the lady, Gresham," the blind locksmith chastised, then paused and added, "Still an' all, I can't help wonderin' what'll become of

31

the Lazy Ladder, Johnny Lutz's spread."

John Lutz, Jessie recalled, was the second victim of the killers who'd made the attempt on Red Greene's life.

"I wouldn't want to say f'sure," the deputy answered. "So far as anybody can learn, John didn't leave any kinfolk or owe any money to the banks or nothin'. Chances are the county will sell the spread for taxes—that's all that's owed on it, accordin' to the reports, and that isn't over much."

"Reckon it'll go to the highest bidder," Bunce said. "It's a good spread, y'know. If I weren't blind, I might've been tempted to bid on it."

Stepping from the boardwalk, they angled across toward a large nondescript barn set back from the main street. It was clear to Jessie and Ki that Thurlow Bunce was perfectly capable of making his way about town, no doubt from years of past memory of its landmarks and the uncanny skill which blind men acquire as a result of their affliction. He made faster time, however, if a guiding hand, such as Winters', was ready to steer him past unsuspected chuckholes or away from unruly horses.

"Well, I've a notion the price won't be over high," Winters said, and turned to Jessie. "Most folks in this section are sort of land poor. They ain't got much ready cash to put out, and they wouldn't hardly sell stock above the regular season turnover to get money to buy more land."

Bunce nodded. "I rec'lect Lutz settin' a high value on his outfit, and that's natural enough, but I never agreed with his idea that this section is going to increase in value real soon. Y'see, Miz Starbuck, Lutz believed in the railroad comin' this way, just as Egg Ainsworth of the Crosshatch opines. I don't. I figure it'll be many and many a year before a railroad gets interested crossin' this section."

Jessie gazed thoughtfully at Bunce, but made no comment while they headed across the lot that extended out around the rear of the barn. It was a dump of old empty barrels and crates, broken wagon parts, and similar trash. In the midst, looking oddly out of place, loomed a sun-bleached cabin with lamplight glowing through the shade of the front window.

"If a railroad ever does come, it'll pass through Spots," Winters predicted. "But if they should take a notion to build to the west of here, the only routes they could take would be over the Lazy Ladder's west range or Ainsworth's east range. So whoever buys the Ladder will be settin' purty, with a fifty-fifty chance plus a sure increase in land value."

Bunce gave a skeptical shrug. "It won't happen in your time, Gresham, or in mine. An' if an' when it ever does, no railroad will pass up the opportunity of routin' through a town."

"Here we are," Winters said, guiding Bunce up onto the front stoop. The door was ajar; from inside came the odors of fried steak and potatoes. Winters opened the door wider and stepped inside the one-room cabin, which consisted of a potbellied stove and pantry shelves in the far corner, a bureau and an unmade bunk bed along one side, and a table and cane-bottomed chairs along the other wall. At the table sat Ichabod Hullinger, spurred boot heels hooked over the scuffed rung of his chair, his gnarled fist gripping a tin cup, looking sourly at the plate of food before him.

"Hey, Sheriff!" Winters said in a loud voice. "You got visitors."

33

Jessie and Ki paused at the threshold of the cabin, expecting the grizzled old star-toter at the table to respond to his deputy's greeting. Instead, he kept staring at his meal, not even brushing away the bluebottle fly that crawled unheeded over his handlebar mustache and hawk-beak nose.

"Dang your mangy hide, wake up! I, ah . . ." Winters' voice trailed off into a shocked whisper. Light from the kerosene lamp on the table caught a ruby droplet, which fell like a dropping bead from a necklace to land on the splintery floor behind the sheriff's chair. Staring, the deputy—and then Jessie and Ki—saw the little puddle of scarlet there, with flies feeding at its rim. It was blood!

Thurlow Bunce dug his fingers nervously into Winters' forearm, sensing the deputy's alarm. Behind his smoked glasses the blind man's eyes glanced up, as if staring at the sudden bone-whiteness of Winters' rotund face. "What's wrong, Gresham?" he asked, whispering through some instinct, as if he knew they stood in the presence of death. "Why don't the sheriff answer? Is he here?"

Winters licked his tongue across dry lips and disengaged himself from the blind man's grasp, sidling warily around to the back of the sheriff's chair. From that angle he had a clear view of what Jessie and Ki couldn't see from the doorway—the handle of a butcher knife, its ten-inch razor-edged blade driven through Ichabod Hullinger's broad back where the suspenders crossed, impaling him to the thin veneer panel on the chair back.

"Gresham! Sheriff!" Bunce called out, waving his arms in sudden alarm and catching hold of the door casing. "Why don't somebody say somethin'?"

Winters reached out as if to touch the knife handle, in the manner of a man who refused to believe the testimony of his own eyes. By now Jessie and Ki had crowded around, and there was no doubt in their minds as to Hullinger's death. The butcher knife's point jutted through the sheriff's calfhide vest.

"Sheriff Hullinger's dead," Jessie said gently to the blind man. "Somebody stabbed him in the back."

Bunce stiffened as if from the impact of a blow. "No, it can't be! I was here with him less'n an hour ago, fit as a fiddle! Help me . . . to a chair," he asked piteously. "This news . . . makes me sick inside. Sheriff Ike was my best pard. Is there one of them . . . notes . . . anywheres around?"

Ki grabbed another cane-bottomed chair and slid it over beside the doorway, guiding Thurlow Bunce into it. Meanwhile, Jessie and the deputy started looking around, dreading what they might find. Jessie found it: a piece of pulp paper resting on one corner of the bureau, weighted down with a shotgun shell. She handed it to Winters.

"Yeah. There's a note, Thurlow," Winters announced, scanning the piece of paper. "Just like the others, typed on newsprint."

"Well, read it to me, you idjit! What's it say?"

Winters cleared his throat. Like a newspaper headline, set in Condensed Gothic, the message read: SHERIFF HULLINGER MADE THE MISTAKE OF IGNORING MY WARNING.

As Winters finished reading, a hush descended in the cabin, and for a long moment the only sound was the monotonous buzz of insects. This was the third time Montana Territory had felt the vengeance of the unknown killer—or killers—who invariably warned intended victims beforehand of their approaching doom, giving them a chance to leave.

"Ten to one the sheriff got left a warnin' to skedaddle, but if he did, he never tol' me," Deputy Winters complained. "If he had, maybe I could've—"

"And maybe I could've helped him somehow m'self," Bunce agreed dolefully, looking like a malevolent owl in his dark glasses. "But we can't go blamin' ourselves, Gresham. He never let on to nobody he'd got it, I bet. That was Sheriff Ike's way, y'know, keepin' things close to his vest."

Winters nodded, sighing, and turned to Ki. "Grab his feet. We'll take him over to the funeral parlor," he said, removing the knife from the back of the chair, then hoisting Hullinger by his arms, careful not to get splattered by blood. The deputy and Ki carried his body out, moving awkwardly and slowly, the dead weight swinging laxly between them. Bunce linked his arm in Jessie's for guidance, and together they followed, Jessie pausing on the front stoop to close the door behind them.

The deputy had given the death note to Jessie for her perusal, and now as she walked with Bunce she reviewed the piece of paper and thought again of the warning note Hullinger's granddaughter had sent to her. It, too, had been printed in Condensed Gothic type, which, unlike handwriting, offered no clue to the sender's identity. The killer's first warning had been brief, sinister:

LEAVE MONTANA PRONTO
OR FACE MY VENGEANCE.

A difference in the second note, however, was that there was a malformation in the letter Y in the word "my." The piece of metal type that the killer had used in setting up this note had evidently been damaged, for the upper right arm of the *Y* had a series of nicks in it that had not taken ink. And as they headed along the boardwalk she saw that up the main street a bit was a small newspaper and job-printing shop. Under her breath she murmured, "I wonder . . ."

A crowd was beginning to collect by the time they reached the funeral parlor. In their shocked faces and strained voices Jessie and Ki read the affection with which the locals regarded the doughty old sheriff. As well came a seething anger, but it had no outlet. There was talk of lynching, but it died aborning against the stone wall of anonymity that surrounded the identity of his murderer. After all, how could anyone hang a killer who was nothing more tangible than a piece of paper with printed words on it?

The funeral parlor turned out to be a storefront operation, the store windows painted with ornate cherubim and the like, and the name HEAVENLY GATES MORTUARY * AMBROSE ZONNEVELD, PROP. fancily scrolled across the top. From within, a tall, cadaverous man in a black fustian coat and stovepipe hat came to the door with a lamp in hand; he held the door open while they brought the body inside, then locked the door against the gathering throng. "This way," he intoned, and they guided Hullinger through a draped archway into a back room, where they slid him onto a metal-clad table. Nearby was another table, cluttered with instruments, towels, and a washbasin. Stacked to one side were cheap coffins of raw pine, but displayed on sawhorses was a more expensive casket, painted gold and sporting bronzed iron handles.

"This's what happened, Ambrose," Deputy Winters began. When he was done explaining how they'd found the sheriff back-stabbed in his cabin, Winters turned to

Jessie to say, "Mist' Zonneveld is not only our mortician, he's also our county coroner hereabouts, in charge of death certificates, coroner's juries, and such."

"I think it's fairly cut-and-dried here," the funereal-looking man declared, studying what remained of Hullinger. The lamp shed a vapid glow that seemed to accentuate the gloom of the back room, and there was a pungent odor, a cloying mix of embalming fluid and rose water that gave Jessie the willies all that much more. "Yes," Zonneveld said, "it's homicide by person or persons unknown, and that's how I'll enter it—"

He was interrupted by a loud, persistent knocking on the rear door. When he went and unlocked the door, a young blond woman in whipcord riding breeches and cream-colored hat tried to push by him and enter. Jessie knew immediately that she was a blood relative of the dead sheriff. Her eyes were the same blue as Ichabod Hullinger's death-glazed orbs, and the classic planes of her facial contours bespoke a hereditary link with his craggy features.

Deputy Winters moved to the doorway, shouldering Zonneveld aside, his blocky form completely filling the opening, cutting off her view of the corpse on the table. "You can't come in, Flora. Your grandpa . . ." His voice choked off, overcome with emotion.

"I heard, but I didn't believe . . ." The girl brought a clamped fist to her mouth, her eyes dilating as she read the horror in the deputy's face.

"Take her away, Gresham!" the blind man spoke harshly. "Take her away afore she gits an attack o' the vapors and faints!"

It took a strenuous effort by Winters to coax the girl to go with him, away from the rear of the funeral parlor. Since there was nothing more they could do there, Jessie

38

and Ki left by the same door a few minutes later. Bunce was with them; he declined their offer to see him back to his locksmith shop, saying he could get to his room over the shop on his lonesome just fine, thanks. He started off in that direction, cussing to himself.

Standing thoughtfully on the boardwalk, Jessie remarked to Ki about the malformation of the letter Y in the second note. "I think a call on the printer up the street might pay off. Anyway, it's a start."

"While you're busy charming the printer, maybe I'll drop in the saloons here," Ki said. "I doubt I'll pick up any information, but like you say, it's worth a try. I'll meet you back at the hotel, okay?"

They parted, Jessie crossing the street and heading up to the ramshackle building that housed the print shop. A large placard propped in the window read WEEKLY GAZETTE PRESS * AMBROSE ZONNEVELD, PUB. "Busy man, this Mr. Zonneveld," Jessie murmured, and finding the front door open, she entered.

Inside was a typical frontier print shop. A herd of cows could have bedded down on the scrap paper that littered the floor. A counter partitioned off the business office, which consisted of a layout table, chairs, coatrack, and a curtain-top desk on which stood a brass nameplate engraved OSRIC NOONAN. Noonan, Jessie reckoned, must be the print-shop manager and editor of the *Weekly Gazette*. Behind the counter was an area crowded with stone-topped composing tables, a rickety flatbed press powered by a rusty steam engine, an alley of type cases, a paper cutter that had a blade like a guillotine, and wall shelves piled with paper stock, glue pots, drums of ink, and other miscellany.

Receiving no answer in response to her call, Jessie decided that Osric Noonan was probably out gathering news about the sheriff's murder for his next edition. If so, she had time to do a little nosing around on her own. So going behind the counter, she went to the alley of type cabinets and checked the labels which identified the font of type contained in each compartmented drawer. About midway through, she located a narrow drawer labeled CONDENSED GOTHIC UPPER CASE in sample printing that was identical to the style of type used by the killer.

Pulling the drawer open, Jessie looked over the complicated arrangement of compartments containing the letters of the alphabet, punctuation marks, em quads, and other type. And not being familiar with the setup of a case of type, it took her several minutes to find the square box which contained around a dozen specimens of the letter *Y*. It was but the work of a moment to learn that her hunch had paid off: one of the *Y*'s had a damaged upper right arm.

Jessie slipped the damaged piece of type into a pocket, slid the drawer closed, and turned—to find herself staring into the business end of a Dragoon Colt. Pointing the revolver was a stockily built man in his late fifties, a man wearing a compositor's ink-stained apron. A green celluloid eyeshade was thrust back over a balding, shell-pink scalp.

"Lady, is you a journeyman printer," the man snarled, "or a thievin' female trespasser?"

"You'll be Osric Noonan," Jessie said. "I . . . I'm sorry. As a matter of fact, I wanted to get some stud-horse bills printed up, and I was going through your type to see what style I thought would look good."

"I'm Osric Noonan," the editor acknowledged, his face purpling with anger. "And if you were a man, you'd be a dead man if'n you didn't get out of here pronto prontico. I don't stand for strangers meddlin' around my shop."

Realizing that it would be dangerous to anger the editor further, and having accomplished what she had come for, Jessie smiled apologetically and beat a hasty retreat out the front door. Osric Noonan, still glowering with rage, followed and stood on the boardwalk holding his revolver until Jessie vanished inside the Ritz Palace Hotel, a block down the street.

To her surprise Jessie found the late sheriff's granddaughter, Flora Hullinger, waiting in the lobby. In the short time since Deputy Winters had escorted her from the funeral parlor the young woman had changed into a black silk dress with flowing skirts and puff sleeves in token of her mourning. In contrast to the sable hues of her dress Flora's throat resembled ivory, and her face, pale under its tan, seemed as delicately modeled as a rare old cameo.

Other than the brief glimpse at the parlor, Jessie had not seen Flora, who was within a year of her own age, since they were pubescent children. Now they greeted each other with much warmth and tenderness.

"I'm so sorry we got here too late to talk things over with your grandfather," Jessie said. "But is there someplace we might go to talk—alone?"

"I'd invite you over to the boardinghouse where I live," Flora replied, "except that the Widow Goldstein doesn't allow visitors in the rooms. There's a courtyard garden out back of the hotel, though, that should allow us some privacy." She led the way through the lobby and out a rear door, and paused and glanced carefully around the dark, hedge-walled garden where the fragrance of rosebushes cloyed the night air. "I don't think anyone's within earshot here, Jessie."

Jessie, too, cast a long look around and up at the hotel windows; then, at least momentarily satisfied, she said, "Flora, I understand your grandfather had his hands full of trouble recently."

"Considerable trouble, Jessie. There've been attacks and rustling going on, and Gramp thought it had the look of an organized business. The ranchers and drovers who've been preyed upon have lost patience and increasingly their tempers, as can be expected under the circumstances, but it's resulted in a lot of brawling and a few shootings and stabbings here in town."

"Did Ichabod have any suspicions as to who's behind the rustling?"

Flora shook her head, her face a pale oval in the starlight as she struggled to control her emotions. "That's one he really wanted the answer to. Of course, every slick-iron gent in the territory has been getting word of how things are up here and has been swooping in to make a kill. That's to be expected. But all the raids that have been made appear to be carefully planned out and pulled off accordingly."

"Where do they run the livestock?" Jessie asked. "Rustled cattle or horses aren't any good unless you have a market for them. This doesn't look like very good country to hide big herds in."

Flora threw out her hands in an expressive gesture. "They run them somewhere, and utterly out of sight. Maybe down Wyoming way or north into Canada. Gramp was never able to discover where they were being driven, Jessie. He was completely baffled by the rustlings, just as he had no idea who this mysterious killer could be. If Gramp suspected anyone, I'm sure he would've discussed it with me. We were very close."

Jessie decided on another angle. "Did Ichabod have any enemies?"

"Gramp could count everyone who knew him as a friend, Jessie, except . . ."

"Except?"

"Well, except for Las' Chance. His real name's Lester, but everyone calls him Las' instead of Les, for short, because he owns the Gilded Lily Saloon here. Y'see, there've been so many shooting scrapes in the Gilded Lily that Gramp threatened to padlock it and banish Chance from Spots. So they've had words, and Chance even threatened to kill Gramps, but nobody ever took the threat seriously. Chance blusters a lot, but he's never physically harmed a man to my knowledge."

Even though she appeared to be concentrating her every faculty on Flora's low-voiced words, Jessie's senses had picked up an alien sound in the night. Something—a foraging rodent, perhaps—was moving through the tall weeds on the opposite side of the hedge from the spot where they stood. It was a tiny sound, a stealthy whisper of movement almost lost under the noise of nightlife echoing from the main street, but that alien sound rang a warning bell in Jessie's brain.

"Flora," she whispered, moving closer, "don't cry out or let on I'm telling you anything unusual . . . but I think someone's eavesdropping on us from the other side of the hedge."

Flora stiffened, holding her breath as Jessie eased her pistol from her holster.

"I want you to drop flat on the ground, without warning," Jessie whispered. "Just in case our prowler spooks and tries something. Understand?"

Nodding, Flora asked, "When?" her whisper betraying a slight tremor.

"Now!"

As she spoke, Jessie did a froghop to one side, moving simultaneously as Flora Hullinger flung herself to the ground and lay motionless, her black dress making her invisible against the grass of the yard. There was a hissing sound behind the hedge, as the unseen prowler gasped a breath across his teeth. For just a second, moonlight silhouetted a wide-hatted figure crouching behind a bush, one arm drawn back as if in the act of throwing something. Then the moonlight made a long silvery streak as a hard-flung knife blade sped arrowlike over the top of the low hedge, aimed straight as a bullet toward Jessie's chest.

Instinct caused Jessie to twist her body sideward, dropping to one knee in the same motion. The eavesdropper's knife shaft grazed her temple and thudded into the bole of a tree behind her, the blade twanging like a plucked harp string.

Flora stifled a cry of alarm as Jessie crashed headlong through the thin hedge. But no shot rang out; only the swift drumming of the knifer's feet, sprinting around the corner of the hotel in getaway. By the time Jessie got to the corner of the building, there was no way of telling which way the knifer had gone. The night had swallowed him.

Flora was still lying on the ground when Jessie returned. Helping Flora to her feet, she said, "Whoever it was got away." Striding to the tree, then, she tugged the knife from the bark. It was embedded a good six inches in the wood, its blade honed razor-sharp. The knife was not a bowie, but almost as large and similar in shape, with the telltale design of the blade that marked it as a Black.

"Why, that's Gramp's!" Flora exclaimed. "The prowler

44

must've stolen it from the cabin when he murdered Gramp." She seemed weak and wobbly on her feet.

Jessie took Flora back through the rear door of the hotel into the lobby, where she bid her good night. "You've had a frightful day, and the best thing for you now is to rest. Don't say anything about this little trouble. If you need me, I'll be up in my room, number fifteen. Ki's staying next door, in room seventeen. And believe me, Flora, we're not leaving Spots until this killer has been caught."

★

Chapter 4

Earlier, while Jessie was walking up to the print shop Ki headed for the main square, where the town's two saloons stood facing each other. The fancier was called the Gilded Lily, an ornate, painted structure with stained-glass windows and the only brick facade in Spots. But Ki chose to first try the nearer of the two, which was simply called PIERCE'S—according to the crudely lettered plank-board sign on the entrance overhang— a combination barroom and trading post, which was comprised of four low, shedlike barns linked by ramps and boardwalks. The trading post part advertised supplies for HUNTERS, TRAIL OUTFITS, AND SURVEYING PARTIES; another sign pointed toward the rear, where there were stables plus big corrals in which were horses and mules for sale. Along the front of the saloon were signs bragging of CUT-RATE PRICES and EVERY HOUR A FREE ROUND.

Entering the establishment, Ki found it to be a scene of contrasts. The woodwork was raw and unpainted, the long bar was made of roughly planed planks, yet the tables and chairs were polished smooth with age and use, and the backbar mirror was genuine French plate.

47

Bottles of every shape and color pyramided the backbar, and the lunch counter over to one side groaned under the weight of beef, ham, cheeses, bread, pickles, and other foodstuffs available at no charge. A derby-hatted man at an out-of-tune piano was batting out a lively jig, while under oil lamps hanging from exposed rafters pranced boozy-eyed gents and their saloon-supplied partners.

The owner, whom Ki subsequently heard addressed as Pierce Demming, was sitting in a high chair behind the counter, where he could observe what was going on in his saloon. His beefy torso—clad in a fancy carpet vest, with a thick, solid gold watch chain extending from pocket to pocket, and an open black coat—showed above the counter. He wore a clean celluloid collar and black bow tie. He kept his black mustache clipped, and the dark eyes in his square face were never at rest, flitting from spot to spot. He exuded authority, shoulders well back and of military carriage, as he watched the merrymaking, every bit profitable to him.

There wasn't as much to watch as Demming would no doubt have liked. The customary revelry was lacking in his saloon, the black shroud of tragedy hanging over the customers. Still, there was no lack of drinkers or of turbulence as talk of the sheriff's murder and of other recent crimes aroused the ire of angry, frustrated patrons. The efficient floor men, dealers, and barkeeps, however, succeeded in breaking up trouble each time before it really got under way.

Tempers are getting a mite short, Ki decided to himself, and there appears to be plenty of disagreement. Sooner or later somebody is liable to go a mite too far, and then hell will break loose.

At the moment two wranglers at the bar were complaining the loudest. Curious, Ki ambled over to elbow in alongside them, overhearing them telling their troubles to the bartender. "Our horses were run off last night while most of us were whoopin' it up here," explained one of the wranglers. "We're from the Double R trail outfit, camped down the line. Left three herd guards, but a big gang of masked thieves killed one and wounded another. They shot down the third feller's mount, drove away our remuda of fifty mustangs. All we had were the horses we were ridin'. Tried to foller, but no luck."

"You don't say," commiserated the bartender. "Which way did the cussed thieves go?"

"North, crossed the river and pushed up the trail, but the sign's lost. Too many hoofs passed by," replied the Double R drover. "Now we figured to get the law onto 'em, but turns out your ol' fart of a star-toter got hisself kilt."

"Don't you disparage Sheriff Hullinger," the bartender growled. "He wore the badge hereabouts for a span of two generations, ever since Spots took root as a trail town. Aw'ri', so p'raps advancin' years had crooked his spine and filmed his eyes, but his gun hand was as sure as ever, and the folks who cast the ballots around here required only nerve and gunslick in our sheriffs. And Hullinger had 'em both." The bartender leaned forward, elbows on the counter. "Tell you what, boys, Mist' Demming will fix you up with mounts at a bargain."

The wranglers, taking the bartender up on his advice, trooped out of the saloon and around to the corrals at the back. Ki sauntered along, keeping a distance, and watched as money exchanged hands and the wranglers left with a new remuda. Then, feeling he'd learned about as much as he was going to, at least for the present, Ki

49

left Pierce's and walked across the square to the other saloon.

Entering, Ki was struck by the comparative elegance of the Gilded Lily. Ponderous hanging lamps of polished brass cast a mellow glow over the room and reflected in the great, mirror-blazing backbar. Hanging prominently in the center of the backbar area was a large oil painting of a nude woman stretched out on a sofa; the painting's frame was gilded, and Ki didn't have to look at the title plate on the bottom of the frame to realize that the Rubenesque nude was named Lily. The floor, cleanly swabbed, was of polished hardwood, in contrast to the sawdust-sprinkled puncheon of Pierce's. One wall was given over to roulette wheels, chuck-a-luck cages, faro layouts, and other gambling devices. There was little gaming going on; in fact, despite the number of patrons, there was a desultory air about the barroom. Obviously the killing of Hullinger had quenched the usual saloon festivities. Indeed, the dancehall, whose shiny maple floor was visible through the archway at the far end of the barroom, was empty tonight. A sign tacked prominently over the archway was readable from the entrance:

NO DANCING WILL BE ALLOWED UNTIL
AFTER SHERIFF HULLINGER'S FUNERAL
Lester Chance, Prop.

Making his way to the polished mahogany bar counter, Ki had no difficulty in finding a place at the brass rail. He ordered rye, and while he was waiting to be served he noticed that standing next to him was Ambrose Zonneveld, the somber-visaged undertaker and coroner. Zonneveld was toying with a shot glass, making wet rings on the bar before him

50

while he conversed with a swarthy, gray-bearded man in rancher garb and flat-heeled boots.

"Yep, the killer must be someone ol' Ichabod trusted real well," the man was saying, "else how could've he gotten close enough to get the drop on him?"

Ki dropped a silver cartwheel on the bar to pay for his drink. Without appearing to do so, he listened closely to the undertaker's reply.

"Between you 'n' me, Jules," Zonneveld remarked, his voice thickened by too much liquor, "Gresham Winters is the gent to watch. As Hullinger's deputy, he could've stood behind the old man and stabbed him in the back."

Studying the men's images in the backbar mirror, Ki saw Jules narrow his eyes thoughtfully.

"Another thing that points to Winters," the undertaker went on confidentially, "is that it's well known that he's been hankerin' to be sheriff for years now. Ever since he lost to Hullinger in the last election he's had a chip on his shoulder the size of a sawlog. Now that Hullinger's dead, Winters is as good as elected sheriff."

Jules shook his head doubtfully. "Winters might've stabbed Ichabod, but that don't account for the killin' of Estleman and Lutz. No, Ambrose, we ain't got proof enough to accuse Winters by a long shot."

Ki moved away, moseying slowly along the bar and then out around the tables, overhearing snatches of conversation by other patrons while thoughtfully sipping his drink. To a man, he found them discussing, in bitter tones, the mysterious killer's latest outrage. Their idle speculations were of little use—just small-town saloon gossip. Everyone in Spots was under suspicion by his neighbors, a fact that was the killer's most potent shield against discovery.

51

Suddenly a frock-coated man began hammering on a billiard table with the butt end of a cue. "Folks, I got an announcement to make," he called out, standing on a chair. "As you all know, the late Sheriff Hullinger was not exactly what I'd call my best friend. We had our differences. But I'm not one to speak ill of the dead or hold grudges."

A hum of angry voices filled the room.

"You better set down afore you say too much, Las' Chance!" Thurlow Bunce snarled from across the room, the blind man leaning against the wall near the entrance. "The whole town knows you hated him. You say anything ornery about Sheriff Ike, and you'll find yourself doin' a strangulation jig!"

Ki eyed the frock-coated man with new interest. Lester "Las'" Chance, who according to the dancehall closure sign was the proprietor of the Gilded Lily, was tall, Lincolnesque in figure, with fish belly–white skin, a clipped mustache, and flashy diamond jewelry. He raised his V-shaped eyebrows, as though alarmed by the hostility mounting against him.

"Don't get me wrong, folks," he apologized hastily, his slim fingers fumbling with the diamond-studded horseshoe pin in his silk cravat. "What I meant to say was that Spots lost a fine citizen when the knifer struck down our sheriff. And I for one plan to do somethin' about it."

A steely silence greeted Chance, but Ki was aware of a subtle change in the crowd. It was obvious that the rich saloon owner was making a bid for the favor of his listeners. Thurlow Bunce groped forward a few steps to a table and, aided by a patron, settled in an empty chair, apparently mollified by what Las' Chance had said.

"Nobody knows who this killer is, or what's his motive," Chance continued. "I want y'all to know that I here 'n' now agree to post a five-thousand-dollar cash bounty at Musselshell County Bank in Roundup, payable to anyone who dabs a loop on this killer!"

Ki nodded to himself approvingly. Money talked in this lawless corner of the Montana Territory. Now that the killer packed a five-grand reward for his topknot, the way had been paved for treachery in case the killer had any friends. More than one outlaw had been betrayed by a confederate for a smaller reward than the one Las' Chance was offering.

"That's all I wanted to say, folks," Chance said, climbing off the chair. "My cash bounty stands till the killer has been brought to justice. For all I know, the sidewinder may be right in this room listenin' to my words!"

Thurlow Bunce grunted and said, "If he is, Chance, you've signed your death warrant. I'll lay odds you'll be the killer's next victim, if you ain't on his list already, and—"

The blind man's words were drowned out by a stutter of shots from outside the saloon, followed by a *clang-jangling* of breaking glass, wild yells and whoops, and a rataplan of galloping hoofs. Again the guns blasted, closer.

There was a howling and cursing outside, and the pad of running boots. A third time the volleying guns roared. The whole upper half of one of the saloon windows dissolved in splintered fragments. Lead whistled through the air and thudded against the wall. A bullet drilled into one of the big hanging lamps, setting it to jostling wildly, a stream of oil cascading from its punctured bowl and spreading on the floor in a swiftly widening

53

pool. The swinging of the lamp ended abruptly as it broke loose from its hanger and smashed to the oily floor. There was a flash, a flicker, then a sheet of flame soared to the ceiling. The guns outside boomed again, and a second window went to pieces.

"It's the MacLoyds!" somebody howled. "They're gunnin' the town! Lemme outta here!"

The front door slammed off its hinges as the entrance was jammed by a cursing, fighting pack of frenzied humanity intent on escaping from the fire that was already licking at chairs and table legs. Somebody fired a wild volley through one of the windows. A stray bullet punctured a second lamp and added its oil to the conflagration. In a moment it seemed that everyone in the room was shooting at something.

Near where Ki stood, around the far end of the bar, was a closed door. He bounded to it, crashed it open with the impact of his hurtling body. It led to an inner room lighted by a single lantern, with a bolted door in the side wall. He shot the bolt, flung the door open, and found himself in a dark alley back of the saloon, an alley that paralleled the main street. Ahead sounded the yelling and shooting, heading for the south end of town.

Gaining on the uproar, Ki raced along the alley. He darted from its mouth, and ahead lay a stretch of open acreage situated between the town limits and a deep culvert. By the light of the moon he could see a band of seven mounted men thundering from town toward the lip of the gully where the trail angled down the bank, crossed the bed, and climbed the other side. And he recalled that when he and Jessie and the Greenes had come to Spots earlier that evening, the roadbed there had been slippery, and runoff rainwater still flowed along the bottom of the culvert. Now, as well as the band of horsemen, Ki saw that perhaps a score of paces behind them rode a tall figure mounted on a big roan. The single rider turned from time to time in his saddle and sent lead hissing back toward the town and the howling, shooting mob that boiled down the main street in pursuit. Ki redoubled his efforts, keeping in the shadow of the low growth that flanked the trail. The riders were not traveling at a particularly fast pace—acting almost as if they were toying with the chasing townsfolk—and he gradually closed the distance.

The band reached the lip of the culvert, vanished over it. The single rider deliberately slowed his horse, turned, and fired back at the town. Behind Ki sounded the deep boom of a Sharps buffalo rifle, just as the tall rider reached the lip of the bank. Ki saw the roan go down in a floundering heap. Its rider was flung from the saddle like a stone from a sling, and rolled down the rain-slick bank. Bounding forward, Ki cleared the edge of the culvert.

A quick glance showed him the crew of seven riders urging their mounts up the far bank, while the eighth man, whose horse had gone down, was kicking and floundering at the bottom of the culvert. Ki leaped down the slope. Just as he reached the bottom, the fallen rider surged to his feet. Black-haired and bearded, he was a giant of a man, his shoulders broad, his chest deep, his arms abnormally long. He wore the homely garb of the rangeland, and wore it with a distinction that set at naught overalls, faded blue shirt, work-marked batwing chaps, and well-scuffed high-heeled boots. Then he closed with Ki, gripping him around the middle with arms like thick rods of iron. Under the frightful pressure of those great arms Ki felt his ribs cracking, his breath exhaling in a gasp. He was all but swung off his feet as the man heaved and wrestled.

At once Ki worked his own arms upward, set his cupped hands under the man's chin, and put forth every ounce of his strength. An instant of terrific strain, a mighty forward thrust, and he broke the grip—but the man, reeling backward, caught his balance and charged with a roar, head low, arms flailing. Stepping aside, Ki chopped the edge of his hand down on the man's nose. The man howled, tears of pain springing into his eyes. Ki followed through by kicking him in the side of the knee, collapsing one side. He caught the man's right arm—crunching down on it with his elbow as he did so—and the man's left shoulder with his hands. Simultaneously, he moved his right foot slightly in back of the man, so that as the man began tumbling sideways, Ki was able to dip to his right knee and yank viciously. His *hizi otoshi*, or elbow drop, worked perfectly; the man sailed upside down and collapsed jarringly in the shallow runoff of rainwater.

Ki started toward him—then hurled himself behind a sheltering boulder as guns blazed on the far bank and bullets hissed and crackled all around him. One cut the sleeve of his shirt; a second burned a stinging welt along the side of his neck. The man on the ground, rolling over, sprang to his feet and ran for the far bank. As the wrathful citizens of Spots streamed down the culvert the man scrambled up the bank to join his companions. There was a final volley of gunfire, a wild yell, and the raiders vanished amid the shadows above.

Ki rose from behind the boulder and shook himself. Instantly he was surrounded by a gabbling crowd.

"That was Bass MacLoyd yuh dropped," someone declared, regarding Ki with an awed expression. Another

56

exclaimed, "I wouldn't have believed there was an hombre in the territory who could knock Bass offn't his feet in a fair fight. 'Pears I figured wrong!"

Ki joined the crowd as they climbed the bank. Back in town they discovered that the fire in the Gilded Lily had been extinguished before it had done much damage. Swampers were packing out smashed tables and chairs. Las' Chance was stamping about amid the wreckage and swearing appalling oaths. Deputy Winters was on hand, and so, too, was Jessie, having been rousted from her hotel room by all the hullabaloo.

"What's this all about, and who're the MacLoyds?" Ki asked.

"They're a sod-pawin', horn-tossin' outfit of hellions," Winters answered. "Ol' Seth is as pizin as a rattlesnake, and his seven boys are wild young mavericks. Sired two sets of twins and a coupla single-draws, Seth did. The one you downed is Bass, the eldest. He's close to thirty, and the he-wolf of the pack. They own the Shamrock Tail spread northwest o' here, kitty-cornered from Red Greene's and borderin' the badlands 'round Flat Willow River."

A bystander, who had the look of a storekeeper, chimed in with aggravation, "Yep, and for some no-good reason, them MacLoyds seem to blame us folks in Spots for the rustlin's they've been sufferin'. Last week they rode into town, in daylight. Bass MacLoyd offered to fight any two gents in town, with guns, knives, or fists. Nobody seen fit to accommodate him. Tonight is a sample of their hell-raisin'. A salty outfit, okay."

"I oughta ride out to the Shamrock and bring the whole bunch back with me and lock 'em up," Winters said with obvious reluctance. "But they didn't do much more'n bust some window glass tonight. Odds are, I'd just end up by making myself look foolish."

"Odds are, you would," Jessie agreed.

"Naturally, if'n I had more to pin on them, I'd foller through," Winters assured her. "There're plenty of folks hereabouts who believe Seth is the headman behind all the owlhootery, but I don't give him credit for that much brains."

"He could be a hot iron in the hands of a man with brains, though," Jessie observed.

"That makes sense, too," Winters said. "Well, g'night."

Jessie and Ki left the town square and returned to their hotel. En route, Jessie recounted her visit to the *Gazette* print shop and her meeting with Hullinger. She handed Ki the death note left with Hullinger's body and the piece of type she'd taken from the print shop, saying as she unlocked the door to her room, "Come on in and take a look at that type and the note, as soon as I light the lamp here."

As Ki closed the door behind them Jessie went to the lamp on the bureau, lit the wick, and set the glass chimney in its brass base. Then, in the act of adjusting the wick, she froze—

"Ki! Look!"

A message had been scribbled in block letters across the bulbous glass chimney of the lamp, letters written with a stub of tallow candle or a lump of beeswax:

STARBUCKERS COME TO SPOTS
AT YOUR OWN RISK.
LEAVE TOWN OR FACE HANGROPE DOOM.

Even as they stared, they saw the waxen letters waver and turn liquid on the heated glass chimney. Then the killer's scribbled warning was a mere wisp of smoke in their nostrils. Cold perspiration beaded Jessie's forehead. Ki, staring closer, saw that the lamp chimney was now crystal clear, but the cloying odor of frying was still in the room as a little beadlet of gray oil dropped down onto the fuel bowl.

"He was here," Jessie murmured. "The killer got in here when I went out to see what was going on, and he . . ." The realization sent an imaginary icicle sliding down her backbone. Whirling, she crossed the room and jerked open a closet door, her pistol in hand. A fusty, cobwebby odor assailed her nose. The closet was empty.

Ki, going to the window, leaned over the sill. Fifteen feet from the wall of the hotel were the weather-beaten clapboards of the abandoned Grand National Opera House, its broken windows staring like sightless eyes in a corpse. Below was the narrow alley between the two buildings. Overhead was a ribbon of Montana sky, powdered over by myriad stars. "He must've had a skeleton key or a duplicate to your room, Jessie," Ki said. "There isn't any ladder down there, that's for certain."

"But how'd the killer know that we've come here because of him?" Jessie asked with mounting frustration. "I've no doubt that the knifer who eavesdropped on me and Flora was the killer. Perhaps he overheard enough to piece things together."

"Perhaps," Ki agreed, turning now to check the note and piece of type Jessie had given him. The comparison left no room for doubt; the imprint of the letter Y in the death note matched the scratched piece of type perfectly. "One thing's for sure. The killer set the type for this note in that print shop."

"In a sense, Ki, finding this clue is almost too easy. And it begs even more questions," Jessie said. "Osric Noonan is the only printer in Spots, and manager of the shop, but did he set the type for this note? Or did Ambrose Zonneveld have a hand in it, as he seems to have in so many things around town? Or is the killer someone else who's got access to the shop without Noonan's or Zonneveld's knowledge?"

"If it's the last, I wouldn't put it past Las' Chance, owner of the Gilded Lily. My first impression of him is that he's a dangerous man, one whose temperament might easily jibe with that of the killer. And it's not uncommon for an outlaw to post a reward for his own capture in cases where his identity is a mystery."

"Ki, it could be any number of people. Even, I suppose, Thurlow Bunce, although it seems a bit farfetched to suspect a blind man. It's not so silly to put Deputy Winters on our list. Certainly Zonneveld thinks he's the killer, according to what you overheard," Jessie shook her head, sighing. "I'm afraid finding our killer won't come as easily as has my discovery of where the notes have been printed. And I've got an awful hunch the solution won't come without blood and mayhem . . ."

★

Chapter 5

Sheriff Ichabod Hullinger's funeral was held early the next morning while streaks of orange, pink, and lavender still highlighted the eastern horizon. A procession to the cemetery west of town was led by Ambrose Zonneveld, who drove his canopied black hearse in which lay the coffin carrying the sheriff's remains. Behind rode Flora Hullinger in a small buggy driven by the Reverend John Flynn, Spots' combination minister and schoolteacher. Then on horseback came Deputy Winters, followed by what seemed the entire population of Spots, including total strangers, eager to pay their last respects to the fallen lawman.

Reverend Flynn, a devout man with a bristly gray mustache and a prominently veined nose, intoned several prayers and other tributes as Zonneveld and his assistants lowered the coffin into the grave. Flora stood as if stunned, her face drained of color, her eyes moist. Nearby stood Ki, his face impassive, although emotions roiled beneath the surface. Beside him Jessie felt a knot tighten in her belly, ready to lash out in a release of sorrow, anger, and frustration—yet strike at what? At whom? Indeed, it was she who was under the constant threat of death from an unknown hand.

When she fell asleep the previous night, Jessie had been wrestling with the mystery of who had written the death warning on her lamp chimney. She had placed her Colt pistol under her pillow, and, as an added precaution, had wedged the back of a chair under the doorknob. A catlike sleeper, she'd figured she'd be roused if the killer put a ladder against the alley window during the night.

Jessie awoke with a start to see the pale promise of dawn making a pink rectangle of her bedroom window. In the ghostly half-light of approaching day the chair propped under the knob looked silly, made her smile with embarrassment. On the other hand, perhaps that precaution had stayed the killer's hand during the night. Dressing, she buckled on her gunbelt and checked the cylinders of her pistol, slipping an extra shell she habitually carried into the empty chamber under the firing pin. Then she went downstairs, where Ki was waiting to accompany her to the funeral.

By then, Jessie had formed an idea of what to do next. . . .

Now mingling with the mourners, she kept her eyes and ears open, avoiding conversations and remaining inconspicuous. After the grave had been filled in and a plain white cross erected at its head, Jessie headed with Ki over to Deputy Winters, who was just walking away from chatting with Thurlow Bunce. Of all the people there, it seemed to Jessie that the blind man was feeling the sheriff's murder most keenly, and as a way of starting a conversation, she mentioned her observation to Winters.

"You may be right, Miz Starbuck," Winters allowed. "Twaz Sheriff Ike who loaned Thurlow the cash to set himself up as a locksmith. They'd known each other long afore a bushwhacker's slug grazed Thurlow's skull and damaged the optic nerves, back when Thurlow was a freighter operatin' 'round this area. He knows it all like the palm of his hand, the only one who'd truck through badlands and backwoods parts overrun with two-legged coyotes, and he paid for it with the loss of his eyesight. I reckon the way Thurlow's courage has overcome his affliction has made him almost as much to the town's likin' as Sheriff Ike."

"I can understand," Jessie said. "By the bye, where is Red Greene's ranch?"

"Wal, take the trail north outta town for a bunch of miles, to the first turnoff west. That'll bring you Loren Estleman's burned out place—"

"Burned out? I thought Estleman was found hanged."

"He was. Whoever strung him up torched his ranch house and barns as well. Anyhow, bear north again, a li'le farther on the trail forks, with John Lutz's spread to your left and Egg Ainsworth's Crosshatch to your right, a big white house settin' on a hill. Go straight, and next along is Greene's place, close to the trail, in a grove of oaks. You'll know you've missed it and gone too far if'n you run into any of them MacLoyd boys, 'cause the trail goes on up, 'round, and across their Shamrock Tail spread. Why? You thinkin' of visitin' the Greenes?"

"Matter of fact, Red invited us out, and I'd like to take him up on his invitation before we leave for home."

That left much to be desired as a detailed explanation, but it seemed to satisfy Winters. "Uh-huh. Wal, you can't get lost as long as you stick to the trail. A mite over forty miles." He turned, then, as Reverend Flynn passed. "A nice service, Preacher."

Nodding dolefully, Reverend Flynn went on to where

63

Flora was standing by the buggy; he helped her in, then climbed in himself. Zonneveld was already at the reins of the hearse. As soon as he wheeled it about and headed out, the Reverend and then everyone else began leaving the cemetery and returning to Spots. Jessie hesitated a moment before mounting her sorrel mare, her gaze on the broken country to the north.

Ki, already asaddle, said, "Okay, 'fess up. What's behind your notion to go visit the Greenes?"

"Wouldn't want to disappoint Violet. She sort of took a shine to you," Jessie replied teasingly, and then grew serious. "Last night Flora told me her grandfather thought the rustlings and raids were planned out, well organized. That would mean an overall plot, not simply random strikes by outlaws on the rampage. And that got me to wondering about the killings of Estleman and Lutz and the try on Red Greene. Deputy Winters confirmed my suspicions just now when he gave us directions. Notice that all the ranches are to the northwest, clustered in a kind of north-south line, and a pattern like that suggests a land grab to me. So I want to ride out and get a lay of the land, talk to Red about what's going on locally— after all, he's one we know for sure can be trusted—and see if we can't find some clue to who's behind all the trouble, and why."

Together they went back to Spots and then headed out of town on the main wagon road north. They rode steadily at an even pace, like travelers who have a long trip ahead of them, as the road twined in and out of steepening culverts and ridge-flanking woods, flexing toward an increasingly tumbled country of staggered slopes, creek-bottom gulches, and dense stands of timber. As far as they could tell, there was no sign of humans, friendly or otherwise. But when they reached a high point, they stepped off-trail and thoroughly studied the ground they had traversed. The road stretched empty to the cluster of toy buildings that was the town.

"Reckon we're not wearing a tail," Ki said as they turned their horses northward again.

Shortly after noon they came to an intersection in the road, where a secondary wagon trail angled off westerly—the trail that would take them to Greene's Rocking-G Ranch if Deputy Winters' instructions were correct. Turning onto it, they followed its deeply rutted track across stony knolls and rough breaks, although increasingly the landscape consisted of pocket meadows dotted with cattle or horses.

The sun was well into midafternoon when they sighted the black blotches that marked the site of Loren Estleman's torched ranch buildings off to their left. The wagon trail snaked rightward, bearing northerly through rock outcrops and thick groves. They let their wearying horses set the pace along the trail, while they constantly surveyed the terrain ahead, on both sides, and behind. It was just past sundown when they reached a broad knoll where the trail abruptly split three ways, with the main track continuing straight ahead. The lane that cut away to the west had a signpost planted beside it; to the signpost was nailed a large wooden board carved wit the Lazy Ladder brand and the name LUTZ. The lane to the right, they saw, wandered down off the knoll and then up another slope to a big ranch house atop a hill, where it commanded a comprehensive view of the surrounding terrain.

They paused at the fork, discussing what to do. There was still a traveling period of afterglow, but they both doubted that'd give them enough time to reach Greene's Rocking-G spread before night overtook them. And considering the threat against Jessie's life, they didn't care much for the idea of riding around in the dark. Besides, their mounts were tuckered out, their chests heaving on every grade and, more than once, their footing going astray. A full day in the saddle had left Ki aching to the bone, and Jessie had the appearance of a woman from whom all energy had been drained.

"If I'm not mistaken, that big house would be the Crosshatch ranchstead," Jessie said. "Let's see if we can't take a breather there, at least to give the horses a rest. They need tending."

Angling onto the lane, they curved down the knoll and through a grove that stretched partway up the hill. From there it was fairly open, and soon they could make out the ranch proper. There was a big barn, bunkhouse, cookshack and mess, smithy shop, and several corrals grouped on the far side of the main house, all dark and silent when they pulled up in the ranchyard. The ranch-house door opened, and onto the porch stepped a squat, ungainly figure holding a cocked Henry repeater at the ready. The burly old gent with truculent eyes and long grizzled beard, Jessie surmised, would be the Crosshatch owner, Egg Ainsworth.

"That's far enough!" Ainsworth shouted gruffly.

Obediently they reined in and sat quietly, calmly eyeing Ainsworth.

Their steady gaze seemed somewhat disconcerting to the ranch owner, who shifted his feet and fumbled with the lock of his rifle. Finally he demanded, "What in blazes do you want?"

Jessie ignored the question, saying instead, "We thought this section was part of Montana. Guess we were wrong."

"A female person!" Ainsworth blurted. "Couldn't tell

in the man's getup you're wearin', not in the dusk."
He cleared his throat. "Yep, this is Montana Territory.
What's eatin' you, woman? You loco?"

Jessie slowly shook her head. "Couldn't be. No, this
couldn't be part of Montana. I never heard of a Montanan
turning hungry wayfarers from his door when it was
getting dark."

Ainsworth glared, gulped, forgot about his rifle, and
reached up to give his whiskers a vicious tug. "I . . . I,
uh, you . . . Oh, thunder! Light off and come'n in. You'll
hafta put up your horses yourselves, though. Ain't a
godda-goldurned waddie left on the place."

Smothering grins, Jessie and Ki dismounted and led
their horses to the nearby stable. As soon as they had
stalled the animals and made sure that all their wants
were attended to, they made their way back to the ranch
house. The front door stood open. Going in, they found
themselves in a big main living room, from which a
staircase led to the upper floor. From the rear of the
house sounded a banging and clattering of pans. They
passed through a second door, crossed a wide dining
room, and entered the kitchen.

Egg Ainsworth, his riotous beard bristling, was
blowing up a fire in the cast-iron cookstove. He
glowered over his shoulder at Jessie. "You'll hafta take
potluck. I ain't no great shakes as a cook. Been livin'
mostly off canned beans for the past few weeks."

As evidence of Ainsworth's lack of culinary prowess,
the kitchen, though comfortably appointed, was a mess.
Shelves and cupboards were well stocked, however.
Jessie, shuddering to herself at the thought of eating
whatever the rancher might offer, turned to him and
said, "If you and Ki will clean up here and wash the
dishes afterwards, I'll fix us dinner. I've been known

to handle a pot or two with fair to middling success."

An hour later they sat down to an appetizing meal Jessie had prepared. Finally Ainsworth pushed back his plate with a long and satisfied sigh. "First decent s'roundin' I've had for so long, I forget when," he declared. "Ma'am, I don't know where you and your sidekick come from, but I'm sure glad you got here."

Jessie, thanking him for his compliment, poured a cup of steaming coffee, and then observed, "It appears things are sort of unsettled in this section."

Ainsworth's reply was a torrent of near profanity and a scorching diatribe against unregenerate bandits and ungrateful crewmen. Jessie and Ki sat drinking coffee thoughtfully in silence until the spasm had ended in a coughing fit that left Ainsworth gasping and speechless— but far from expressionless.

Jessie eyed him for a moment and then remarked, "Boiled down to low gravy, I gather what you're saying is that your crew was scared off by a warning you got."

"You betcha! A warnin' note, just like poor ol' Estleman and Lutz got, to clear out or meet my maker."

"And Red Greene got," Jessie added, and explained the circumstances leading up to Greene inviting her and Ki to visit the Rocking-G.

"Don't that beat all," Ainsworth growled, shaking his head. "Wal, there's one difference betwixt me'n Red. He had the sense to keep his old hands on, slow an' old as they'd gotten. They'll stick, no matter what. Me, I got smart and hired on a hotshot bunch of young 'un's who up an' abandoned me at the first whiff of unpleasantry. Somethin's gotta be done, but durned if I know what." Ainsworth glowered and muttered, stoked an old briar

68

pipe with black tobacco, lit it, and puffed on it harshly. At length he burst out, "Stay over t'night, will you? I lay awake all night, thinkin' and listenin' and startin' up at every stray noise. I reckon I'd sleep better if you were here."

"Hope so," Jessie replied enigmatically. But as she finished her coffee and waited while the men washed the dishes a concentration furrow was deep between her brows, a sure sign she was doing some hard thinking.

"I sleep on the second floor. Miz Starbuck, you can take the guest room right across the hall from mine, and Ki, your room's at the end of the hall," Ainsworth told them. "That useta be my foreman's, dad-blamed him!"

The bed in the guest room was a comfortable one and boasted clean white sheets. Jessie did not open it, though. She spread a blanket on top and removed only her boots and gunbelt before stretching out. Her pistol she placed within easy hand's reach. Then she lay quietly gazing through the window across the room. The night was overcast, but moonlight seeped through the vapory mantle, casting a ghostly glimmer over the rangeland. Jessie could dimly make out the gloom of barn and bunkhouse. Right around the hedge of tall brush that fringed the ranchyard, however, it was very dark. A light wind had risen and soughed sadly through the shrubbery, making a heart-chilling music.

Jessie drowsed from time to time as the hours passed, but she never fully slept. Suddenly her eyes opened wide. Above the moaning of the trees she had caught a sound, a small but sharp and metallic sound, such as is made by bridle chains when a horse petulantly tosses its head. Tense and alert, she lay listening. The sound was not repeated, and gradually her eyes closed once more. They snapped open as a voice rang out, insistent, compelling. "Ains-s-sworth! . . . Egbert Ains-s-sworth!"

Following a moment of tingling silence, Jessie heard the old ranch owner's feet thump on the floor as he sprang out of bed, grumbling curses. But before Ainsworth could open his door, Jessie, her gun buckled in place, stepped out into the hall. Ki was already there, wide awake and fully dressed, and when Ainsworth emerged with his Henry in hand, Ki gripped his shoulder before the rancher could storm down the stairs.

"Hold it," Ki said quietly, the struggling Ainsworth helpless in his grip. "Hold it! You're snapping at bait."

Ainsworth relaxed, but he still mouthed curses.

"Down the stairs quietly, now," Jessie told him. "Keep out of line with the window."

"I know what that yell means," Ainsworth grumbled. "The hellion's callin' me out to talk through smoke. He don't hafta call twice."

"And you'd have about as much chance as a fart in a tornado," Ki said. "Shut up and do what Jessie tells you. Can't you see there's a loop spread for you?"

They reached the lower floor, and again the voice beckoned, "Egg Ainsworth! We're coming to git yuh!"

"Tell them," Jessie instructed, "to go to hades, but stay here, out of line with the window."

Ainsworth told them, adding some choice descriptive phrases to the request.

"Watch the window," Ki murmured. "I think there's someone standing alongside that big bush out there. Watch close, but don't pull trigger till we tell you to."

"Here we come, Ainsworth!" the voice shouted out. At the same instant Jessie, staring diagonally through the window, glimpsed a flicker of light in the direction of the bunkhouse.

Something dark and flapping came hurtling toward

70

the ranch house. Jessie held her pistol at arm's length and fired two quick shots. Instantly the crack of her gun was echoed by a salvo of slugs that whistled past her, Ki, and Ainsworth and slammed into the far wall. There was a chorus of exultant yells outside the ranch house. And at that moment the flicker by the bunkhouse soared upward in a rushing sheet of flame. By its light could be seen a number of men running toward the ranch house. Behind them were mounted men. Instantly Jessie triggered her pistol again. Egg Ainsworth's Henry boomed like thunder.

One of the running men was stopped short, as if by a giant hand. He whirled, sagged to the ground, and lay still. A second pitched headlong in a sprawling heap. A third wheeled drunkenly for the shelter of the oaks. The voice that had tried to lure Ainsworth outside now bawled out, "Outta here! Hightail outta here!"

A tall, muscular figure leaped from behind the big bush, fired a volley at the house, and turned to run. Jessie's pistol cracked twice. The tall leader's hat whirled from his head, exposing his thick ebony hair. Then he was gone among the shadows. A bullet from Ainsworth's rifle and the last slugs from Jessie's pistol whined after him. A moment later the sharp click of racing hoofbeats sounded, fading swiftly into the distance.

"Looks like they got a hideful," Jessie commented, ejecting the spent shells from her pistol and replacing them with fresh cartridges. "Come on. We've got to douse that blaze before it gets away from us!"

Ten minutes of hard labor extinguished the fire. The flames, crackling from a large bundle of oil-soaked brush, hadn't had enough time to get much of a hold on the bunkhouse wall.

"She'd have been going strong in another few seconds,

though," Ainsworth said, mopping at his perspiring face. "Now let's drag those punctured lobos over to the house and give 'em the once-over."

He paused to pick up the hat Jessie had shot from the tall leader's head. It was a brown J.B. of good quality, but when examined in the light, it disclosed no identifying marks. Nearby was found a loosely folded slicker, likewise devoid of markings. The two dead raiders were strangers, although as Ainsworth pointed out when examining them, "Mean lookin' jiggers, ain't they!" Their pockets yielded a miscellany of articles of no significance, but both carried thick wads of bank notes.

"Folding money," Jessie mused, leafing through the notes of large denomination. "I imagine you don't see much of it in this area, do you?"

"No sirree bob," Ainsworth confirmed. "Makes me think that these gents came from the outside." He stared intently at the hard faces of the slain raiders. "Their boss, y'know, he had a lot of hair black as coal-tar ink, didn't he?"

"Looked that way," Jessie allowed.

"There's only one big tall jigger I know of in this section who's got hair like that," Ainsworth said slowly. "Bass MacLoyd, of the Shamrock. I dunno . . . it don't seem to make sense. I can't figure the MacLoyds havin' anythin' to do with banditry of this sort, but that feller was mighty like Bass in build and height, and had black hair."

"Lots of big tall men have black hair," Jessie said. "That man didn't have to come from around here, you realize."

Ainsworth nodded, as if half hearing. "The MacLoyds are a wild bunch, okay," he continued, "but I dunno.

72

Old Seth usta be almighty salty when he was younger, but he 'pears to've cooled down considerable of late years. He was born and brung up in this section. A good many years ago he pulled out for a spell, then come back drivin' a big herd to stock his spread. Never had much to say as to where he got that herd, and naturally folks did some speculatin'. Seth was always a tight-lipped cuss, and he 'lowed his business was nobody else's. Right, I reckon, but it does start folks to talkin'. Rumor-mongerin' has it that the boys do some slick ironin' and such, but nothin' was ever proved agin any of 'em. Nope, I dunno, but that jigger did have plenty of black, black hair." Ainsworth paused, then went on in querulous tones. "What in blazes would they gain by such hellishness? They're owners, too!"

Jessie said nothing. Neither did Ki; they both appeared deep in thought.

"I heard tell that ol' Seth figured to bid on John Lutz's property when it comes up for sale," Ainsworth suddenly added with apparent incognizance.

"According to what I've heard," Jessie said, "there seems to be differences of opinion over just how valuable the Lazy Ladder is."

"Yeah, and that depends whether or not you believe the railroad will be comin' through thisaway. Me, I don't much subscribe to that notion. It's only been this year that the Utah & Northern Railroad has reached Dillon, and best estimates are that the Great Northern won't cross Montana for another three years. Ain't no doubt that sooner or later a branch line north into Canada will be built, but to my way of thinkin', it'll be later. Good'n later."

"Excuse my asking, but if you'd been killed tonight, what would've happened to the Crosshatch?"

73

Ainsworth grunted. "Reckon I'm in the same stall as Lutz, in that respect. I got no kinfolk I know anything about."

Jessie nodded thoughtfully, then glanced at Ki, who was heading back out toward the shrubbery. In answer to her quizzical glance, Ki said, "I want to look over the ground under the bushes. Another man jostled off like he was hard hit, and maybe he's lying out there. And there might be a stray horse or two. Brands sometimes are important."

"Chances are all the horses were bein' held, and they took the light ones along when they vamoosed," Ainsworth said. "But that plugged jigger went off like he was powerful sick, so p'raps we'll find what's left of him."

A careful search of the ground proved Ainsworth right about the horses. There was no sign of the wounded raider until Ki discovered where the held horses had waited. The sky had cleared, and the moon was shining through brightly now, and by its light they found blood spots trailing off down the hill.

"Headed north by east," Ki said, "at least when they left here. May turn off some other way later, of course."

"Think you might track 'em by that blood?" Ainsworth asked.

"Not much chance, even if it was daylight," Ki replied. "Either the bleeding will stop shortly or the guy will cash in. Either way we'd be out of luck."

Jessie nodded agreement. "The best we can do now is to go back to bed. I doubt there'll be any more trouble tonight. We'll cover these two bodies with a blanket and bury them in the morning."

"Wish I had some tame buzzards to take care of 'em," Ainsworth growled. "It'd save us the work. . . ."

★

Chapter 6

Next morning, after Jessie and Ki helped Egg Ainsworth bury the two dead raiders, they saddled up and headed back along the lane toward the wagon trail. However, as soon as they were in the grove at the bottom of the hill, out of sight of the Crosshatch ranch house, they cut off the lane and circled around through underbrush and boulders until they were roughly in line with the rear of the ranchstead. There they began a methodical search for tracks of the raiders' mounts, and shortly, where the ground was still boggy from the recent rains, they intersected a morass of fresh imprints of shod horses. The churned earth clearly showed that a pack of riders had passed here en route up the hill and then back down, the marks returning northward whence they came.

Jessie eyed the tracks as they continued on through the grove to a dry, flinty rise upon which hoofs left no sign at all. "Can you follow them?"

Ki shrugged. "I wasn't fibbing last night when I told Ainsworth that we wouldn't have much chance." He then grinned thinly. "I guess we weren't fibbing, either, in *not* telling him we wouldn't go try."

"Poor Egg," Jessie said, sighing. "I don't like misleading him, but he'd have insisted on coming along. That'd have been too risky—for us all."

From the flinty rise the tracks curved northwesterly through a forest. For a time Ki was able to read the sign without dismounting, for there was scarcely any underbrush. The woods were a mature stand of huge conifers, uniformly sized and widely spaced, rising straight and branchless to great heights before their tops unfurled. Soon they crossed the wagon road. Jessie could hear birds chattering from bowers along the shoulders, but once back under the high canopy of trees, there was silence. It made the forest seem impermeable and eternal and made her feel ephemeral and insignificant. Eventually, the imposing stand softened into a landscape of average groves, stone ledges, and rough brakes.

As Ki worked out the tracks Jessie rode cautiously, checking all round—particularly scrutinizing their back trail. They were, after all, following a course traveled by the killer gang, and it could very well be that the outlaws would be along this path. But there was no sign of others as they rode for the better part of the day, and at length they descended into a region of knuckled hogbacks, sprouting thatches of briar and bear grass, and stone benches like arid plateaux. Some of Ki's tracking was done by instinct now, once going a half mile along a gully before he found that his intuition had been good. A white scratch, the iron of a horseshoe against a rock; a stepped-on twig. . . . But mostly he followed logic and experience, a combination of knowing the line of travel taken already and of sensing where it would most likely continue.

So far, the raiders had been heading more or less northwestward, their greatest variations being around

76

or through difficult terrain. There was nothing ahead that appeared menacing enough to avoid or attractive enough to turn for. So Ki kept them moving straight— or as straight as the jagged landscape would allow— toward tawny mountains that cut the horizon like teeth of a blunted saw.

Nearing the base of the foothills, they came upon a path that was thread-thin and rarely used, that wound generally in the same direction. When, presently, they paused at a small gulch that bisected the path and was perhaps two spans deep, Ki's hunch was confirmed. The gully's far edge was indented with a hoofprint. It hadn't yet crumbled in on itself, and still showed signs of where the hoof had overturned some of the gravel, indicating that it was made within the last twenty-four hours. It was enough.

The path wandered through a succession of interconnecting valleys and canyons and eventually entered a long valley full of boulders and treacherous underfoot. Tracking became impossible again, to the point that Ki reined up when the valley emptied into a centuries-dry riverbed. The bed made an eroded and rubble-strewn trail of sorts leading back into the broad rise of hills, where it most likely snaked higher among mountainous cliffs and chasms.

"I hate to admit it, but I think they've lost me," Ki said. "On the other hand, they were heading for the mountains, and there isn't another accessible pass anywhere within miles, leastwise that I can see."

"Well, it's just the sort of badlands jumble that outlaws would use," Jessie observed. "In fact, that worries me some. We'll be hard to miss."

True enough. They pushed on, meandering across the heat-blasted foothills through a maze of connecting gulches and ridges. Eventually they emerged along the eastern rimrock of a gorge that stretched like a raw wound cut through the mountainous heights. Riding on, more or less flanking the rim of what was really a great sunken ravine, they noticed that in places the gorge walls fell sheer, and in others the walls dropped in slopes of crumbling shale and rock slide; and all the while the gorge kept opening out, like an ever widening funnel, until it was miles wide and very deep. Shadowy, mysterious, with stands of pine and other growth, its floor, Jessie realized, formed an ideal cattle range that nature had fenced in with walls hundreds of feet high.

Finally they saw, far up the ominous gorge, a mighty spire of naked rock soaring high above the distant stony walls. Veined and ledged and turreted, its towering height swathed in shadows like purple mist, its circular crown of apparently bare rock shimmered in the late afternoon sunlight. Jessie gazed at it as they continued paralleling the edge of the gorge, and as she gazed, her brows drew together in a perplexed frown. From the crest of the spire, faintly staining the blue of the sky and fouling the crystal-clear air, was a thin streamer of bluish smoke.

"Ki, look there— Am I imagining things?"

Staring where she was pointing, Ki shook his head. "No, it looks like that rock is a hollow chimney with a fire lighted at its base. But that's nonsense. It's solid rock, if anything ever was."

"And nobody could climb it, that's for sure. Even if they could, who would? And to light a fire on top?" Jessie gazed more fixedly at the pillar. No, there was nothing on its top. She could see clear across it to the western rim. Nothing moved within her view, not even a soaring eagle that might have a nest there. But still the tiny plume of smoke rose into the air. She watched it until it thinned and vanished, leaving the air clear and translucent. And still the sunlight streamed from west rim to east rim of the gorge, without a shadow to break its sweep. Well, she hadn't imagined it; both Ki and herself had seen the smoke rising from the top of a rocky butte impossible to climb. It didn't make sense, but it was so. She shook her head and rode on with Ki.

Abruptly she was recalled to her immediate surroundings as Ki twisted in his saddle and called to her sharply, gesturing behind and to their left. At the edge of wide and dense thicket to the east, a half-dozen men were riding out of the brush and streaming swiftly toward them.

"Ki, Do you think they're—"

Jessie's question was interrupted—and answered—as a puff of whitish smoke mushroomed from the ranks of the approaching horsemen. Before the crack of the report reached their ears, something screeched through the air above Jessie's face. Instantly she and Ki raked the flanks of their mounts, launching them into a hard gallop before the pursuers could close near enough for accurate shooting. Chances were, Jessie figured, that the men were outlaws, members of the same gang who had raided Ainsworth's ranch the previous night. But she had no intention of sticking around to ask, any more than Ki had.

Then, suddenly, it appeared that escaping wouldn't be an option—perhaps half a mile diagonally ahead and to their right was another bristle of growth extending over a wide area; and out of this area rode another band of men, nearly a dozen of them, Jessie estimated. With loose rein and busy spur they swept toward her and Ki. Even before they were within rifle-reach, they began shooting.

Jessie and Ki glanced at each other, exchanging worried looks. Clearly they could not turn back because of the riders behind them. There was only one way to go; turning their horses, they headed for the edge of the gorge. Above the drumming of their horses' irons they could faintly hear the exultant whoops of the pursuit, for they were trapped between the two groups and the ragged rimrock. They reached the gorge lip. Its massive wall dropped sheer to the brush-grown floor hundreds of feet below. The group to their right was farther from them, so they rode along the rim in that direction. A bullet fanned Jessie's face; another twitched at Ki's sleeve like an urging hand.

Jessie fingered the butt of her saddle carbine. The Winchester was a last resort. All she could hope for, if it came to a showdown, was for her and Ki to go down fighting, taking as many of the outlaws as possible. The odds were too great against them to expect to shoot their way out. Her eyes swept the terrain ahead, and abruptly brightened with renewed hope.

"Ki! There!"

"I see!"

Less than two hundred yards distant was a jagged gash in the rim. Here the wall had in some far distant age suffered a gigantic rockfall. A ragged slope of talus stretched steeply to the gorge floor. Broken, seamed, jutted with boulders, tufted with growth, it was an appalling route to safety, but Jessie and Ki instantly decided it was their one and only chance.

Goading their horses yet faster, they closed the remaining stretch to the rim and launched over the side. The horses squealed in protest, hunched their hoofs, and took a sheer drop of ten feet or more before landing on slipping, sliding shale. Somehow they kept their footing and went storming down the almost vertical slope. Rocks rolled under their hoofs; clinging brush tore at them. Banks of shale slid downward in an avalanche of dust and flying fragments. Erect in their saddles, Jessie and Ki steadied and guided their flying mounts with voice and hand. Bullets stormed through the dust clouds. But their motion was so erratic and the angle so difficult, that it was more or less like shooting at sunbeams playing tag with lightning flashes.

Ahead was the gorge floor, still very far away. Behind was a roaring avalanche of earth and stone and displaced boulders. The long slope stretched on and on, like the upended teeth of a gigantic barrow, with the horses crashing from point to point, seemingly doomed to disaster at every leap. Dimly Jessie and Ki realized that the yelling and shooting were far away, growing farther. Another moment and they were drowned by the roar of the rock slide thundering at the very heels of their horses. Boulders whizzed past them, striking the slope below, bounding high into the air and hurtling on, accompanied by shoulders of fragments and puffs of dust. Behind was a sickening grinding sound as great masses of earth and shale joined the avalanche. The air was thick with dust and stinging grit.

Ki set his teeth grimly, and Jessie braced herself for the crushing impact of the rolling wave that would any instant engulf them. Then suddenly she gave a cry of triumph. She felt her sorrel's irons crash solidly on level ground. Out of the dust cloud shot her horse, Ki's moro gelding a neck behind, hoofs drumming. With a crashing roar the avalanche hit the gorge floor, but the thunder of its arrival was well behind the flying horses.

They did not pull their mounts in until they were beyond rifle range. But when they glanced back through

81

the thinning cloud of dust, the rimrock was empty of life.

"Decided not to hang around, eh?" Ki observed.

Jessie nodded. "I hope so. Now, where are we?"

Red Greene's Rocking-G spread, she knew, had to be considerably south of the gorge. From their present position she could see the gorge splitting the mountainous badlands into a section to the east and one to the west; however, that strange, tall spire of a rock formation was no longer visible.

Finding no reason to turn back—and perhaps risk another run-in with those outlaws—they headed north at a leisurely pace. A couple of miles farther on, they threaded their way through a stand of pine, oak, and alder. Emerging from the final fringe of growth, they saw, less than a hundred yards distant, a huge black-haired man riding toward them. An instant later Ki recognized the rider as his antagonist in the ruckus at Spots night before last.

"Why, that's Bass MacLoyd!"

Bass peered at Ki and Jessie, his neck out-thrust, his fierce gray eyes intent under scowling black brows. Suddenly he let out a roar of recognition and spurred forward.

"Wal, set me afire!" he bellowed. "The jasper I had the wring with. I been wantin' to meet up with you again, wantin' to mighty bad!" Bass MacLoyd's truculent bellow ended in a roar of laughter as his freckled face seemed to split from ear to ear in a white-toothed grin. He thrust out a huge paw as he pulled his horse to a slithering halt alongside Ki. "Put 'er there! I hanker to shake hands with the only jasper I ever met who could knock me down. No hard feelin's, and I hope you ain't got none either. Put 'er there!"

82

Ki put 'er there. Their hands clasped in a steely grip, and they grinned into each other's eyes. Bass then doffed his hat as Ki introduced him to Jessie, and again bellowed laughter.

"Did we bust window glass in that pipsqueak town!" he roared. "I ain't had so much fun since paw got his whiskers caught in the corn sheller. And that shindig you 'n me had finished it up proper. The way them townsfolk throwed lead at me was a caution, but they never could shoot up in Spots. I felt bad about my horse, figured he was done for. But he was just creased and skalleyhooted across the ditch a little farther down. Caught up with us before we'd gone far. Say, I heard tell we set the Gilded Lily on fire. Haw! Haw!"

Even Ki's habitual reserve thawed in the warmth of this black-thatched gray-eyed Scot. He chuckled reminiscently.

Bass regarded them both with mirthful eyes. "Say, whatcha all doin' here in the gorge? How'd you get down?"

"We came by way of that rock slide a couple of miles south."

"By way the rock slide!" Bass repeated. "You mean you rode down that slide?"

"Sort of," Jessie admitted. "Though I think we were in the air most of the time."

"You sure must've wanted to get down almighty bad. Say, that wouldn't have to do with that shootin' I heard a spell back, would it?"

"It would." In a few terse sentences Jessie explained why they were so anxious to reach the gorge floor.

"Don't know what things are comin' to in this section," Bass growled, shaking his head. "Gettin' so it ain't safe for an honest man to ride across the range. Well, come along with me to our castle. The boys and the Old Man will be glad to meetcha proper."

After Bass neck-reined his roan around, they headed together on up the gorge. Shortly, on their left, they saw a stream fed by a pool worn into the bedrock, and the pool, in turn, was supplied by a waterfall tumbling hundreds of feet from the lip of the gorge. Instead of staying on the left, the stream slewed toward the middle of the gorge, where it curved to flow northerly, in the same direction as they were riding. They joined a path that generally flanked the stream, and began threading through conifers and box elders and thickets of creepers, around house-sized boulders and across patches of slabstone and rubbled slag. And unceasingly, Jessie and Ki surveyed the terrain, doubly aware after their narrow escape from the gunmen that each gap, fringe, and thicket was a potential menace, each point along the rimrock a possible vantage for eyes and gunsights.

So, not surprisingly, they were somewhat relieved when, presently, Bass cut away from the stream on another path, led them to the eastern side of the gorge, and up a serpentine trail to the gorge rim. From there they crossed a long stretch of rugged rangeland to the Shamrock Tail ranchstead—a long, thin, cabinlike ranch house; a squarer bunkhouse, against which leaned a grub shack; a clapboard barn and a scattering of sheds; and a pole corral, in which a few horses stood. The Shamrock spread did not look rich, Jessie thought as they approached the bare yard in front of the house; but it was neat, and the buildings appeared to be in good repair, indicating a desire to work hard and to the best with what there was.

A gallery ran the length of the ranch house. There was a small amount of clutter and discarded saddlery at each end of it, but in the middle, next to the front door, was a rocking chair. Sitting in the chair was undoubtedly the patriarch of the MacLoyd clan, "Old Man" Seth, wizened, cantankerous, with filmy eyes and a complexion like tanned leather. He wore a loose-hanging vest and denims of the range, a faded bandanna knotted around his throat, a thatch of white hair peeking from beneath a floppy-brimmed, sweat-stained hat. The elder let out a whoop, and from the house and around the yard appeared his six other sons. A few minutes later Bass was introducing Jessie and Ki to bre'ers Mish, Tully, Glin, Doyle, Lorne, and Ennis. It seemed to Jessie that each was bigger than the other, though none quite equalled the giant Bass in height or bulk.

"Glad there's someone can slap Bass down," Seth said to Ki. "Hell knows he needs it. It's a pity you didn't use a singletree on him, only the chances are that head of his woulda busted the tree. C'mon in! C'mon in! It's time to eat."

As the female guest of honor, Jessie was escorted to a chair next to the redoubtable Seth. And she couldn't help wondering as the MacLoyd clan took chairs around the large dining table if ever there was a time around here it *wasn't* time. The table groaned with food, and the carnage that ensued was ferocious, for their appetites were gargantuan. But their tongues worked as merrily as their teeth.

"We have times t'gether," Bass remarked to Jessie. "I'll ne'er forget the time when Lorne and me went inter the Gilded Lily and found paw settin' in a chair and hollerin' like blazes. Swore he had creepin' paralysis. Couldn't move his legs. Lorne hauled him outa the chair and lifted him clean outa his boots. Him an' his creepin' paralysis! 'Pears while Paw was drunk and asleep, Ennis had nailed his boot soles to the floor. Him an' his creepin' paralysis!"

Ennis shook in his chair while old Seth struggled not to blast out a string of profanity.

Dusk was falling by the time the meal was finished. The western rim of the distant gorge glowed with strange and wonderful fires. Great shadows crept across that wide sunken canyon toward the east wall that still glowed golden in the reflected rays of the vanished sun. Then these, too, dulled and darkened until the vast fissure was brimful of shadows, above which the stars glowed like golden spear points thrusting through a canopy of blue-black velvet.

Somewhere from the depths of the gorge sounded the lonely plaint of a timber wolf. An owl perched high in a pine answered with a querulous whine. Somewhere a coyote yipped to the coming moon. A whisper of wind stirred the grasses and mingled with the pungent odor of cedars and box elders. Tully MacLoyd began thrumming the strings of a guitar while Ennis and Glin got rigs on their horses.

"They're due to nighthawk the big herd we got bedded o'er on the range," Bass explained. "Maybe we're bein' foolish, ridin' guard way over there, but so many things have happened of late that're we're a mite jumpy."

Jessie nodded her understanding; undoubtedly, there was a wave of fear sweeping the central Montana rangeland. Soon all save Ennis and Glin retired for the night. While Ki bunked down with the boys Jessie was shown the guest room, where she slipped naked into the comfortable bed, feeling the crisp sheets delightful against her bare skin as she relaxed, shutting her eyes. Sleep claimed her quickly.

A tentative knocking on her door awoke her.

"My God, is it morning already?" she murmured blearily, and shifted around, tucking the sheet to her neck. "Who is it?"

A muffled, "Er . . . Um . . . Ah . . ." came through the door.

"Oh, it's you, Bass. Come on in, the door's unlocked."

The door eased ajar, and Bass MacLoyd slid inside, quietly closing the door behind him. He was wearing a striped nightshirt that was far too small for his muscular frame, and coming only to his knees. "I . . . I didn't mean to disturb you."

Jessie didn't respond at once, but struggled to sit upright with the sheet draped modestly around her. Bass was hesitantly padding closer, the short nightshirt twisting about his muscular legs as he moved, emphasizing his crotch area. And watching him with sleep-dimmed eyes, she thought dizzily, either Bass's got his gun on under there or he's hung like a horse!

Her errant thought caused a slight twinge of self-consciousness to steal through her, and she hastily glanced higher—only to see Bass's eyes roaming the contours of her thrusting breasts. "Yes. Well, was there something you wanted, Bass?"

"I can't sleep."

"And you don't want me to sleep, either?"

"Oh, no, I . . ." He sat down gingerly at the edge of the bed. "No, I wanted to talk, Miz Starbuck—"

"Jessie, please."

"Jessie. I was tossin' and turnin' and just knew I'd never catch a decent bit of rest until I explained to you."

"Whatever about?"

"Well, you must have a plumb awful opinion of us

87

MacLoyds. Don't blame you, after the way we tore hel—heck outta Spots t'uther night and then filled your head with rowdy yarns t'night."

"Why, I don't think badly of you at all."

"Nice of you to say so, Jessie, but truth is we ain't very genteel. Maw always tried to pound some manners into our thick skulls, and on occasion it took, but since she died of consumption some years ago, we've kinda sunk into ungentlemanly habits. We don't mean no harm, though, honest."

Bass stood then, stiffening his shoulders as though preparing to face a firing squad. Instead, he was facing a young woman whose view of his jutting loins mere inches away was causing her taut breasts to tingle, her rosy nipples to harden involuntarily. From their first meeting she'd been attracted to the easy grace of his motions, the strong muscles flexing in his chest and legs, the hard bas-relief of . . . Whoops! Jessie scrunched her naked buttocks against the mattress in an attempt to quash the budding tendrils of arousal curling in her belly.

"I feel like a lummox, Jessie," Bass was saying. He paused, his tongue licking his lips as he regarded her . . . and Jessie could sense it now, the desire stirring within him despite his best intentions. He cleared his throat, tried again. "Like a bull in a china shop. And I ask for your forgiveness."

"No forgiveness needed."

"Thanks." He continued standing, rooted uncomfortably.

"Was there anything else you wanted to tell me, Bass?"

"No, I guess that's about it."

"Then for heaven's sake come to bed."

He choked. "Don't fun me, like I was thinking to take advan—"

"No?" she cut in, a ghost of a smile creasing her mouth. "It never crossed your mind, Bass?" She let the sheet fall free of her breasts. "It's crossing mine, and it's crossing yours."

"Guess it shows, eh?" He grinned ruefully, glancing down at his nightshirt perversely tenting out from his loins, and then gazed smoldering at her, his voice husky. "Well, it 'pears I can't deny that if the lady is willin', I wouldn't dislike a kiss 'tween friends."

She gave a long purring sigh. "The lady is willing . . ."

Bass joined her on the bed, kneeling alongside and bending to touch her lips, kissing her gently, almost teasingly. A breath later he was kissing harder, and she was kissing back, and fire was in their mouths. When finally he eased from their soulful kiss, he shifted to suckle each breast, laving each nipple into aching hardness before moving lower to her navel, and then to her love mound, his hands smoothing the sheet away as he wetly progressed.

Jessie moaned blissfully as he parted her legs and slowly laid his fingers upon her rosy nook. "Pink," she heard him whisper. "So pink and moist and tender delicious . . ."

His mouth pressed hungrily against her crevice, his tongue snaking out to lick its full sensitive length, swirling over the tingling center of her womanhood. Jessie gasped convulsively, but Bass gave her no respite, burrowing deeper in a prolonged, forceful kiss, whipping his mouth up and down until her hips trembled and her loins throbbed with kindling orgasm. She felt herself on the verge of release, when Bass raised his head and grinned.

"Now, *that's* kissing," he said, positioning himself between her open thighs. "This boy sure do hanker for tasty kissin'." Quickly removing the nightshirt over his head and flinging it aside, he again smiled carnally as he stared at her splayed, glistening crotch.

And Jessie stared at his exposed erection, trepidation mixing with yearning. "Lord, it is . . . it's big as a horse's!"

"Naw"—he loomed over her, and she moaned, feeling his blunt girth pressing against her anxious hollow, and hearing him add brightly—"but say a colt's, and I'll call it my peacemaker."

"Mmmm . . . I imagine that depends on how you spell it," she quipped, her moan becoming a quavering groan as he began to enter slowly inside her. "I think it should be called a widowmaker."

Chuckling, Bass lunged.

Jessie sucked in her breath, eyes widening and mouth gaping, shivering from the ecstatic force of his stabbing penetration. She feared she'd cry out and bring the entire MacLoyd clan running before he was totally buried within her. God, he was filling her! And to relieve the strain she spread her legs wider, still quivering as she continued to feel herself stretched by his massive shaft.

He started pumping, tunneling deeply, furiously, hammering her savagely. And she was responding with equal savagery, her breasts trembling to his surging assaults, her internal muscles clinging tautly as he pounded rampagingly far up into her belly. Jessie could feel every tiny fold of her squeezing with each stroke of his spearing manhood, her hips pistoning to match the rhythmic batterings of her flesh, her buttocks grinding lasciviously against the tempestuously rocking mattress.

A tremor began gathering inside her, a warning like the advance of a sundering avalanche. Frantically she raced to meet it, her motions skewering her completely around his plunging shaft. Again she poised breathless, tensing, straining . . .

"Ahhhh . . ." She bit her forearm to keep from screaming, her nails raking furrows in the bedsheet. She felt Bass shudder and his seething volcano erupt into her spasming belly. Then gradually they fell limp, Bass remaining burrowed in her, becoming flaccid yet still feeling very large to her.

Jessie hugged him when, withdrawing, he pressed close beside her. She stifled a contented yawn, tired as ever and satiated to boot, her sensual fires banked and cooled. She closed her eyes.

And dozed.

This time nothing, not even the loss of his warm body when Bass gently arose to depart, could interrupt her deep slumber.

Not until dawn was peeking through the trees, that is. It was then that Jessie was startled from her sleep by a clatter of hoofs outside the ranch house and a yell. She slid out of bed, padded to the window, and peered out. In the dim light she could just make out the bulky form of the rider. Something was draped across his horse's withers. Alarmed, she dressed hastily and was out on the porch almost before Ki and the half-clad MacLoyd boys poured into the yard.

The rider was Glin, his eyes wild, his face blood-streaked. The unconscious man in front of his saddle was his brother Ennis. "Shot through the shoulder," Glin panted. "Lost a lot of blood. Went outta his senses on the way here. I got creased, knocked stupefied. When I come to, they was gone, the herd, too!" And with that,

91

Glin flopped out of the saddle with all the grace of a falling sack of potatoes.

"Them sidewinderin' skunks!" Seth bawled as his sons carried Ennis and Glin into the house.

Jessie went to work on Ennis as soon as the man was laid out on the couch. With delicate, skilled hands she cut away his blood-drenched shirt and bared the bullet wound in his left shoulder. "The bleeding has nearly stopped, and no bones broken" was her diagnosis. "He should pull through all right. Get me hot water and soft rags and something to use for a bandage. The bullet went clean through, I'm glad to see. We'll have him patched up in a jiffy."

"Ma'am, you should've been a doctoress," Seth declared, beaming.

As Jessie straightened a few minutes later and inspected her bandaging she said, "He'll be waking up pretty soon. When he does, give him some warm milk with a little whiskey in it, and keep him quiet. No, I don't believe there's any hurry for a doctor. We'll get one from town later, if there's one there."

"There is, an old feller named Kunkel," Seth grunted. "He's gettin' rich of late. Doc's a first-rate sawbones, though."

Jessie nodded, her eyes narrowing slightly. "Now, Glin, it's your turn." Quickly she cleaned and bandaged his wound, which was relatively trifling.

"Everything busted loose just afore daylight," Glin then explained, "right when it's the darkest. Me 'n' Ennis met ridin' around the herd and stopped for a smoke. Just as I struck a match I thought I heard somethin'. Then the sky fell down on me and I saw a lot of stars and it got black. When I come to, the herd was gone. Ennis was layin' under his horse, groanin' and bleedin' bad.

I hauled him out and got him on my horse and headed for home. He was mumblin' and mutterin' for a while, then he got still. I was scairt he'd bled to death."

"You didn't see which way they went with the herd?"

"Didn't see nuthin', Paw."

Jessie turned to the other wounded MacLoyd. Ennis's eyes were fluttering. A moment later he opened them and glared wildly about, swore, and tried to sit up. Jessie quieted him and gave him the warm milk Mish had prepared. Then Seth asked his youngest son the same question he'd asked Glin.

"They headed west with the herd, a dozen or more of 'em," Ennis whispered. "I saw 'em ride off before things started to get hazy for me. That's all I know."

"Looks like they might be headin' for Eagle Perch," Bass said.

Jessie glanced quizzically at him. "Eagle Perch?"

"Don't tell me you 'n' Ki didn't see that great big tall hunk of rock pointin' heavenward when you was nearin' the gorge. You couldn't have missed it."

"That's Eagle Perch? I can understand where it got its name."

"Yeah, and the whole gorge is named after it." Bass stroked his chin, then turned back to his brothers. "If them wide-loopers 'er headed for Eagle Perch Gorge, we've got 'em. There's no way outta there."

"Wal, git goin'!" Seth snapped. "They may've figgered that both the boys were done for, and they'd have plenty of time!"

★

Chapter 7

Minutes later Jessie, Ki, and the MacLoyds were heading across the range. Old Seth remained at the house to look after his wounded son. Glin, despite his bandaged head, had insisted on accompanying the others and, with Bass, was leading the way, the rest stringing after them, weapons ready for instant action.

They reached the spot where the herd had bedded for the night. Marks of it were plain and they followed the trail with little difficulty. Bass's guess proved correct— the trail of the stolen herd led down a shallow drift into Eagle Perch Canyon and then northerly along the stony, brush-choked floor.

"We can't take no chances on an ambush," Bass pointed out. "It'd be just like a salty outfit to hole up here somewheres, figgering we'd come chargin' after 'em. If they get the drop on us, they'd mow us down like sittin' quail."

But as they progressed, the gorge remained silent and deserted. The MacLoyds, trained rangemen, searched the terrain with keen eyes, alert for any movement in the brush. Jessie's and Ki's gazes rested mainly on the crown of growth, because the gorge was full of birds and they knew that the presence of men in the brush would be sure to set the birds acting up.

The growth began to thin somewhat, and ahead towered the massive bulk of the Eagle Perch. Its base was set in a dark and sinister-looking niche choked with water-worn boulders and a bristle of trees, which grew thickest along the shadowy battlements hemming it in. Approaching, Jessie measured the towering spire from its base on up to its peak. Its sides were curiously ledged and seamed, but up close she could see no more sign of striation on the stony walls than she'd been able to perceive at a distance yesterday. At the same time, her curiosity was increased as to the source of the streamer of smoke she had observed rising from its lofty crest then. She shook her head as she gazed at the perpendicular walls.

"Somebody might possibly make his way down from the top if he were part cat, but nobody living could climb that thing," she commented to Ki.

He nodded. "Even if a guy had a reason for climbing it, he'd have to be loco to try such a stunt." Calling over to Bass, he asked, "Ever been up top?"

"You figger I got wings under my shirt?" Bass retorted. "Nobody ever climbed it, I reckon, and nobody's ever likely to. Why?"

"Just wondering. You could get a fine view of things from up there."

"Reckon so," Bass agreed. "You could sweep the whole gorge and the range all around for miles."

Riding on, they slowly, carefully combed the silent gorge. As they progressed, the growth thinned somewhat and the floor became stonier, until finally the herd left

96

no trace of its passing. But still the grim walls towered to the sky without a cleft or break.

"They can't get out, that's sure for certain," Bass reiterated from time to time. "We've got 'em trapped."

"If they don't trap us," Glin complained, gingerly caressing his wounded head.

"Got to take the chance," Bass retorted. "Keep your eyes and ears wide open."

They continued on mile after mile into the gorge, with only the birds and an occasional rodent or rattlesnake or two as evidence of life. The tall brush still grew thickly along the walls, where infrequent springs and small streams provided sufficient moisture, but the center of the gorge was barren. The MacLoyd brothers separated and rode the brush on either side, not daring to stick to the easier going for fear of ambush. Finally there loomed before them a towering granite wall that boxed the gorge from side to side. Bass MacLoyd pulled up with a bitter oath:

"Outfoxed, goddammit! Now how'n the blazes did they do it? The only thing I can figure is that they doubled back after making a trail for us to follow. Don't you figure it that way, Ki?"

"Could be," Ki allowed, in tones that carried little conviction. He sat inspecting the end wall of the box, then shifted to study each side. Wordless, he shook his head, his eyes speculative. "I don't know how they did it, but the fact remains they did. It's a smart outfit, okay."

Deciding that there was no sense in staying there at the box end, Jessie, Ki, and the MacLoyd boys turned their horses and rode back down the gorge. The MacLoyds ranted and fumed, but Jessie and Ki were silent, their intent gazes never leaving the terrain ahead. The group was perhaps halfway to where the Eagle Perch reared its lofty spire when Ki suddenly swerved his mount's head to the right.

"Into the brush!" he called. "Quick!"

Jessie, knowing that Ki never warned without good reason, immediately responded. The MacLoyds didn't know what it was all about, but they had sense enough to take Ki seriously. And as their horses hit the bushes head-on, from the growth ahead burst a storm of gunfire. Bullets whined all around them, clipping twigs, smacking against stones. Tully MacLoyd yelled a curse as a slug burned a welt along his ribs. Mish lost his hat. The fork of Lorne's saddle was shredded by lead that missed him by inches.

Deep in the sheltering growth, Ki swung from his saddle. "Easy, now, and quiet," he directed. "We'll try and sneak up on them. If they stick around to see what happened, we may have a chance to get the drop on them."

"Pal, that was close!" Bass grunted as they began to worm their way silently forward.

Behind them Jessie and the other MacLoyds crept ahead foot by slow foot. Nothing moved in the bristle of bushes ahead; no sign broke the silence. As they advanced, they redoubled their caution and were alert for action. Finally Ki held up a warning hand. Wordless, he pointed to something shining in a patch of sunlight that filtered through the tangle of branches—an empty cartridge shell.

"Right here is where they holed up," he whispered. "Easy, now. I've an idea they shifted back a way after shooting."

The slow advance was resumed, but as they covered yard after yard Ki's black brows drew together. He accelerated the pace a trifle, and they covered perhaps another hundred paces until they came to where the growth began to thin. Finally they crouched behind the last fringe of foliage and peered down a quarter-mile stretch where the growth had straggled out to occasional low shrubs. Nothing was in sight. Ki stood up and stepped boldly in the open, protected only by the MacLoyds' covering rifles. Nothing happened. Birds were flitting about, chirping cheerfully. A rabbit hopped along a couple of hundred yards ahead, caught sight of Ki, and scooted for cover.

"Might as well go back and get the horses," Ki said quietly. "Outsmarted again!"

The MacLoyds swore luridly—then apologized to Jessie—and glared down the gorge. Still muttering oaths, they trooped back to where the horses waited, ground-reined.

"Okay, Ki, how'd you catch on to their ambush?" Bass demanded. "I didn't see a thing, didn't hear a thing. They was hunkerin' plumb outta sight, but you knew they was there. How?"

Ki grinned thinly. "Birds."

"Birds!"

"Sure. The birds told me they were there. All the way up the gorge and back down me'n Jessie have been watching the birds. They have been going about their business all the time, until just as we came in sight of that thick clump we were riding toward. Over that thicket a couple of birds were darting and wheeling, acting all nervous about something. Of course, it could've been a snake closing in on their nest or some such, but I preferred not to take any chances. I knew for certain something was holed in that thicket."

Bass drew a deep breath. "And if you hadn't had an

eye on the birds, by now another sort of bird would be driftin' down from the sky with eyes on us and gullets all set for a big feed. I never did fancy to pass out as buzzard bait!"

Reaching their horses, they remounted and continued on down the gorge, proceeding with caution, sticking to the side walls and avoiding open spaces. The MacLoyds were convinced now that the rustlers must have headed south to get out of the box gorge and were eager to press the pursuit in spite of fearing another ambush. Their advance was unmarked by incident, however, and even when they passed the jutting crag of Eagle Perch, which would've provided excellent concealment for drygulchers, nothing happened. Jessie glanced back at the somber spire, now shimmering in the sunlight. It seemed to her that the ledges and fissures formed into mocking, malevolent faces that leered after them, chortling with unseemly mirth at their discomfiture, as if the strange butte was chuckling to itself at the mystery over which it stood guard.

Finally they reached the gorge mouth. Before them stretched the open vistas of rangeland, utterly devoid of life or movement. The MacLoyds stared about, muttering. Ki narrowly scrutinized the ground at the gorge's mouth.

"O' course, they could've gotten out of sight by ridin' almighty fast," Doyle MacLoyd conjectured, "if they larruped right after shooting at us and had their hosses close by."

Ki said nothing, and continued to eye the ground. "Plenty of marks of cattle and horses going into the gorge," he said at last. "But not one of either coming out. Take a look and see if it isn't so."

Jessie took Ki's word for it, but the MacLoyds

dismounted and went over the ground. Bass finally swore in baffled exasperation. "You're right," he grudgingly conceded. "But if they didn't come out, where'd they go?"

Ki shrugged his shoulders. Nothing could have been more thorough than his and the MacLoyds' combined examination of the gorge, yet the fact remained that a herd of cattle and a rustling outfit had utterly vanished in its somber depths, apparently into thin air.

"Well, reckon we might as well ride back to the house," Bass suggested. "I guess the meanest chore a man ever has to do is to 'fess to bein' whupped. But they's takin' a whole herd of ours, and there ain't a thing any of us—"

"To where?" Jessie interrupted.

"Howzzat?"

"Where are they taking your herd?"

"*Away,* that's where!"

"No, I mean where's the market for your rustled stock?"

The MacLoyds chewed on that for a moment. It was Mish who finally answered her. "Discountin' Canada, I'd say Fort Maginnis. We've sold them plenty of beef recently and have a standing order to supply 'em military mounts. Yep, I'd say the fort."

"All right, assuming the rustlers headed your herd that way, would they likely travel any particular route, stop at a particular water hole?"

"Only one practical way, via Hoss Thief Crossin'," Bass replied. "That's the ford acrost Flat Willow River. Y'see, some decades ago there was an owlhoot trail through these parts. Many a cow has walked it, and word has it more'n one Canadian rancher got his remuda running stock off horsemen to the south of us, only to have other galoots later on spirit the offspring of them cow ponies back south. And that's where Hoss Thief Crossin' got its handle, it bein' part of the easiest grade and shallowest ford across the badlands. It's part of our range now, but . . . Aw, Jessie, it's impossible! Our cows couldn't have gotten from here to that ol' trail!"

"It's impossible your herd got from here to anywhere! But it did, Bass, and I'm only considering where the rustlers would've taken them—once past this little obstruction. Now, do you want to take a chance, or head on home? It's your choice."

Again the MacLoyds mulled things over. At length, Doyle spoke up. "Sounds crazy to me, but no more crazy than losin' the herd here. Y'know, there's that path a few miles from here that's tough goin', but a shortcut for our horses. Cows can't navigate it."

"So can it get us to the crossing before the herd?"

"Hmmm . . ." Bass rubbed his jaw. "We could probably do it. I don't reckon the herd, even shoved damned hard, could make it before we could." His pugnacious face lit with a grin. "Jessie, you done sold me. There's a chance that's the way the rustlers went, and there's a chance we can catch 'em before they ford the Flat Willow. And no matter how slim, that's more chance than we got goin' back with our tail twixt our legs."

They started out. The MacLoyds knew their range like small boys know their own backyard, and they led the way for a grueling hour through jagged rock and raking thorn before intercepting the path that Doyle had mentioned. The path over the badlands proved to be as bad as claimed, and worse. It was undoubtedly very ancient, but was now no more than a faint depression winding amid growth and over ledges, studded with boulders and washed out by rains.

"Nobody much used it 'cept Indians, prospectors, and hunters," Bass said. "Reckon nobody ever uses it now. In fact, only ol' scouts like our Ol' Man who grew up 'round here recollect it bein' here."

"That's all to the good," Jessie responded. "Chances are the rustlers won't know about it either, and it might help us take them by surprise."

The rambling course northwest was hazardous to the extreme. The horses were often blowing hard by the time they reached the crest of badlands' rises, and it was necessary to call halts for a while to enable them to catch their wind. Frequently the descents were even more dangerous, with broken necks being averted by what came close to miracles. The sun sank in the west and evening turned to dusk into night, the blackness compounding their perilous journey. Jessie grew more anxious; the ride was consuming much more time than the MacLoyds had anticipated. But to try hurrying it would be suicidal.

Bass was also growing worried. "It's about two miles before we dip down to Hoss Thief Crossin'," he remarked. "I think we can make it, but we haven't time to waste. We've got to beat them there and find a place to burrow in, or all this ridin' will've been for naught."

Soon the path plunged precipitously, like a curlicue slide. Eventually the badland hills on either side began to fall away, and within another half hour the eroded river valley ahead was visible. The sharp grades of the hills continued to lessen until they met and blended into the gradual slopes of the valley. Though no longer as steep, the path kept sinuously pitching and slewing downward as it skirted the lower flanks of the hills. Soon a draw in the badland cliff could be dimly seen.

103

From its bell-flared mouth a churned earth trail rolled toward the gravel- and dirt-banked Flat Willow River. Ki surveyed the black flowing current below, but could not spy any telltale moonlit glisten of splashed water or wet mud at the point of the ford.

"The rustlers haven't crossed here yet," he remarked. "Assuming we're right, it looks like we may still be in time to catch them on this side of the river."

Heartened, they picked up their pace. Yet between them and Hoss Thief Crossin' was a lengthy slant of shale and boulders, devoid of vegetation. The only practical route across was this rugged and winding track, which they rode at a reckless clip. They were closing to within a half mile of the ford when they glimpsed the van of the Shamrock Tail herd suddenly emerging from the draw.

"Look yonder!" Doyle MacLoyd shouted.

Bass sank steel to his roan. "Rifles!" he bellowed. "Shoot soon's they show, before they can spot us and scatter along the herd. It's our only chance to bag some of 'em!"

The panting horses were sliding and skittering down the bank. Rocks rolled under them; gullies and crevices caused them to flounder. And the cattle were pouring from the draw in a steady flow.

"A thousand yards," Jessie murmured. "Long range for firing from horseback." With one hand she levered her saddle carbine. "But here goes, because here they come."

The last of the cows were through the mouth of the draw. Behind them men on horseback were shoving them along the old owlhoot path to the river. The night silence was broken by the sudden sounds of splashing and snorting, of men calling out and cussing as the van of the herd broke back, reluctant to take the black water.

104

The moonlight showed their blurred, moving shadows.

Bass raised his rifle, his eye glancing along the sights. His brothers did the same. The river valley reverberated with the blast of gunfire. The rustlers whirled, startled, in their saddles. Dazed with alarm, they ducked and dodged as lead stormed around them, and for a moment they seemed to hesitate, milling in wild confusion. Some tried to rally, clawing for weapons. But others, with slugs whining about their ears, were not slow to turn and hunt for cover.

One man, veering from the pack so fast that his hat got swept off, bent low across his horse's withers as he raced for the nearest brush. Ki rode to head him off, keeping a strip of willows along the bank between them.

"Take to 'im, Ki!" Bass yelled.

Another of the MacLoyds whooped, "Git his hide!"

Ki took it at a run, figuring the man would either have to come through the brush toward him or take to the river farther along the bank. Then he heard the splash of water across the willows; the man was taking to the river. He reined his horse into the willows. In a few seconds the big moro was hopelessly tangled up in the brush and driftwood piles.

Quitting his horse, Ki plowed through the brush on foot, the willow branches and wild roses ripping his hands and face. He fought through the thicket, pawing with his hands, his breath coming in winded gasps, sweat bathing him as he wrestled to get through the snarled bushes. He came out on the bank, only to find the open stretch there empty. Out yonder, more than halfway across the river, the man he wanted was getting away. Ki stood there, cussing, then turned to head back, seeing that the rest of the gang was disintegrating into a panicky mob, intent only on hurtling for the safety of the draw.

Yelling, the MacLoyds and Jessie were charging after the rustlers with careless abandon, risking broken bones or death at every stride their horses made. Without accident they reached the trail, swerved toward the mouth of the draw—but they didn't enter it.

They couldn't. The terrified cattle, bawling and milling, had floundered back from Hoss Thief Crossin' until they choked the narrow mouth with a morass of rampaging flesh and bones. Try as they would, it was a good half hour before the sweating, cursing MacLoyd boys could get the entrance clear. And then they headed in after the rustlers.

"Hold it!" Jessie shouted. "Hold it. It's no good. You're risking the same thing you did back in Eagle Perch Gorge. And the rustlers will try the same thing— to hole up and blow us off our saddles."

Bass considered and nodded. "Yeah, back off, boys. We lost our bear meat this time. Maybe it'll be different next time."

Grousing, his brothers complied. With savage looks and brandished fists they turned their horses and filed out to begin regathering the herd. It had not scattered or even spread much, the cattle feeling little zest for moving after two stampedes and a long night's run. Which was good, because even with Jessie and Ki helping hunt and gather strays, an eight-puncher crew would have been no match against a couple of hundred feisty critters. Soon the cows were again bunched in a herd and were trudging wearily eastward along the bank of Flat Willow River. Some miles yonder, according to the MacLoyds, there was a spot where they could turn off and head in a roundabout way back to their grazeland—

106

a pain-in-the-butt drive that would likely take them till morning.

Still, Bass was exultant with relief, chortling over the recovery of the herd and congratulating Jessie on her shrewd deduction. But Jessie was in a bitter mood. She had hoped they would trap the rustlers and capture at least one to question, thereby gaining a lead to the boss of the gang and putting a finish to the lot of them. Instead, as Bass had said, they'd lost their bear meat.

★

Chapter 8

It was the black of deep night, somewhere around four a.m. by the time Jessie, Ki, and the MacLoyd brothers had bedded the Shamrock Tail herd and returned to the ranch house. Old Seth MacLoyd received them with a vivid vocabulary bordering on profanity and caustic comments anent "younkers who couldn't be trusted to do anything right." He dispatched Lorne to town to fetch Doc Kunkel and retired to his armchair beside Ennis's bed to grumble and growl behind the smoke of a cheap six-fer-two-bits cigar. Despite the noxious tobacco cloud, Ennis appeared to be recovering, in weak but uplifted spirits—perhaps due to the frequent generous dosages of milk mixed with whiskey.

Everyone else trooped into the kitchen, where within minutes they were partaking of bacon and eggs, flapjacks, and cups of fragrant coffee. After the meal Jessie and Ki discussed whether they should catch some sleep there or ride on to Red Greene's Rocking-G spread; they decided on the latter, perked up by the coffee.

With a suspicious grayness now in the sky, they set off on the lane that connected the ranchstead with the wagon trail. Traveling the lane and, presently, south along the wagon trail, they journeyed through brush and gulches and flinty hogbacks; but they were also treated to a scan of the Shamrock Tail rangeland that had not been visible yesterday, and they gazed approvingly at the pocket meadows, the numerous groves, and trickling creeks that provided good shade and graze for livestock. Suddenly, however, Jessie gasped and bolted upright in her saddle.

"There! See?" she cried, pointing to a flickery crimson glow climbing the dim sky to the southeast of them. "A fire! It's got to be!"

"It is, and growing awfully big awfully fast," Ki muttered, peering at the feverish burn swelling up across the sky. "Makes me wonder if it had help, like Egg Ainsworth's and Loren Estleman's had help."

"Exactly—but in any case, we can't ignore it!"

Kicking their mounts into stretching runs, they kept them heading along the trail while the blaze inflamed the near distance, radiating a crimson beacon. Across stony flats, through timbered benches and brush-strewn depressions, they rode low over their horses' flowing manes, urging them on. Then for a stretch the terrain flattened to an open tableland that reflected scarlet and ash from the fiery sky.

About a half mile ahead, on an oak-groved low rise a few hundred yards off-trail, they saw fenced ranchground enclosing a two-story house, a barn, and other buildings. The barn was a raging blaze, and the ranch house was burning intensely throughout its whole lower portion with an ember-crackling, smoke-belching roar. Closing fast, they noticed three partly clad men sprawling lifeless by the bunkhouse door and an old duffer in long johns attempting to climb a ladder to the second-floor window

110

at the end of the house. But from a window below gushed increasingly fierce heat and jetting flames, sparking the already smoldering ladder, driving him back each time he tried to mount.

On gut-heaving lathered horses, they reined in by the frantic oldster and dismounted at a run. Jessie called, "Is somebody upstairs?"

"The boss! Both of 'em!" he yammered. "Neither Greene came down!"

"Greene!" Ki shot him a probing look, then glanced at the surrounding grove of oaks—of course, this could be none other than the Rocking-G. "Are you sure Red and Violet are up there?"

"Shore I'm shore! Saw Miz Greene at her window till smoke got 'er, an' she fell back afore she could climb out." The oldster pointed at an upper window by the front of the house, then motioned to another window midway. "Ain't seen Mist' Greene since he went up to bed. But he ain't down here now. Must be up there, too. They're gettin' burned alive!"

Scanning the house, Jessie sighed despairingly. It did seem largely hopeless, Ki, too, had to admit. Downstairs was an inferno, flames erupting and scaling the outer wall almost to the upper windows and blocking access to either Greene's bedroom. Only in the rear was the fire still below the second story, which was why the oldster had put the ladder at the last window. Ki eyed the ladder speculatively; it promptly burned in two and dropped with a crash. Most of the upper windows were reddened, and back of the open one—Violet's window, presumably—a funereal glow was beginning to strengthen.

"Fire eating through the floor," Ki reckoned aloud.

"Stairs can't be used. None of the trees are close

enough to swing up and in from," Jessie added glumly. "There's no outside chimney to climb, no verandah roof, no place possible that I can see. Can you?"

"No." Pivoting, Ki gripped the oldster by the shoulder. "Where can we get rope—say, sixty feet of good lariat? We'll need a crowbar or a posthole digger, too, or even just a shovel with a strong handle."

"Ropes are—were—kept in the big barn, but there's a corral shed for spares. The tools are in a shanty o'er thisaway!" At a bandy-legged trot, he led them to the nearby shanty. "Whatcha got in mind?"

"No time to explain," Ki declared, delving inside.

Jessie felt none too sure she wanted to know. Whatever it turned out to be, his idea was bound to be daredevil risky and, she suspected, so harum-scarum she'd wet her britches worrying.

Ki quickly chose a long-handled spade. Next they hurried to the shed, finding it a snakepit of discarded rope and tackle gear. Furiously they dug apart the rope tangle; the lengths were either too short or too rotten or both, until finally Jessie unwound seventy-plus feet of sturdy manila hemp. They hastened outside, Jessie coiling the lariat, Ki eyeing the fire and then turning to the oldster.

"An ax! Can you get me an ax?"

"I knows where there's a hatchet."

"It'll do. Hurry! The fire's climbing fast!"

Obeying, the old puncher stumped for the bunkhouse as fast as his gimpy limbs would permit. Jessie and Ki rushed toward the house, arriving near the back where the ladder had stood. Double-checking, Ki detected no serious flaws in the frayed, worn rope or any cracks or woodbugs in the seasoned hickory handle of the spade.

112

He noosed the handle in the middle, took a turn and a hitch, and was drawing it tight when the oldster returned, wheezing and stumbling, a broad-bladed hatchet gripped in his gnarled hand.

Thanking him, Ki took the hatchet and thrust its haft in the back of his waistband. He held the spade poised over his shoulder and stood rigid for a moment, gauging distance and angle. Then his right arm snapped forward. The spade hurtled through the air, leading with its heavy metal head, the rope trailing behind. Right through the second-story window it speared, to land on the floor with a clatter that sounded above the roar of the flames.

"Jehosafat—whatta pitch!" the oldster gawked, owl-eyed.

Without commenting, Ki drew the dangling rope taut, whipping the sag up before the flames from the lower window could sear it. As he had figured, the long handle of the spade caught on either side of the window frame and held fast. He dashed to a nearby oak and wound the free end of the rope about its trunk and, with Jessie joining in to pull, drew the length as taut as possible and tied it securely. Then, flashing her a parting grin, he gripped the slanting rope and began going up it, hand over hand.

"I knew it," she sighed. "It's a pisser."

The oldster, divining Ki's purpose, yelled a frantic protest, "The rope'll burn through, and you'll ne'er git down!"

Ki made no reply, saving his breath for the steep climb.

"You'll git caught up there an' roasted, too!"

Jessie advised the oldster: "Save your lungs. Ki doesn't wear ears."

"He do so, I saw 'em!" The oldster gave a snort, then

113

shouted, "They's done suffocated by now, anyway. It's a lost cause, losin' you!"

Now Ki was dangling over the flame-spurting first-floor window. Its furnace-breath seared him, and for an instant his senses reeled. Then he gripped the window ledge, drew himself up to a perch, and, with his elbow, smashed out the rest of the glass. With a heave and a plunge, he slid through the window frame, past the spade handle, and sprawled on the floor.

Regaining his feet, he crossed the room to the door, feeling its panels for heat before opening it. He peered into a corridor that was dimly lighted by the flames that were coming through the floor. The nearby end door, which doubtless opened onto the rear stairs, was closed. Across the hall was another door, and farther along it, a row of four more doors on each side. That matched the number of windows, thank God, making it easier to locate the rooms.

Ki headed up the corridor, counting doors, stopping at Red Greene's room despite his urge to get Violet. Her uncle needed help as much or more, not having even reached his window.

Finding the door locked, Ki jerked the hatchet from his waistband and began chopping out around the latch plate and striker. Splinters flew, the door's frame and panel splitting and crumbling. Soon he had an opening through to the bedroom, and right then and there he knew he was in for trouble. He could hear flames crackling and churning, and rolling out from the opening was thick smoke and blistering heat. Once he got the door open, a volcano of destruction would pour out of the bedroom. He kept on nevertheless, and after some more cutting, he kicked out the latch assembly and opened the door.

Fire and smoke mushroomed out, and the corridor

114

sprouted incandescence. Ki staggered back, choking, eyes stinging, the smoke-boiling air searing his lungs as he thrust to the doorway again. Squinting in, he saw that over to one side was a tumbled bed, as though someone had risen from it hastily, throwing the covers back in wild confusion. In a corner was a burning chair over which hung burning a pair of breeches, a shirt, and overalls. A burning hat rested on the bedpost. Dangling from the post, under the hat, was a shellbelt. The butt of a revolver protruded from the holster. At the foot of the bed stood a pair of smoking boots. The large middle area of the room had vanished; the floor had collapsed. Fire was blossoming up like a disease through the hole, consuming the bedroom with avid hunger.

Red Greene was beyond rescue.

Lunging on along the stifling, smoke-reeking corridor, Ki located Violet's room near the front stairs. The staircase was gone, and the stairwell groaned from the ominous roar and crackle of the fire rushing up from the furnace below. Her door, too, was locked. With all his strength, he hacked and hewed, grimly aware that at the other end of the house, more flames were swelling upward, drawing ever closer to his thin manila line of escape.

After what seemed an age, Ki smashed enough to force open the door. The bedroom was more or less intact, missing no great chunks, though the floor was afire in places and fumes were sifting between the boards. Through the seething murk he could dimly see Violet in her peignoir nightgown, a motionless huddle slumped on the floor below the open window.

He started crawling toward her, choking in the supposedly clearer air near the floor. He rose to a crouch and shoved on through the clouding smoke, and after an eternity of blind groping, his hands encountered her limp body. He held her wrist and found the thready beat of her pulse.

"Hang on, you're going to make it," he murmured to the unconscious girl. Whipping out his bandanna, he found her wrists and bound them firmly together. Then he stood up, gasping in the heat, and looped the bound hands about his neck. Violet was inches shorter and pounds lighter than he, but she was no picayune featherweight, either. Carrying her piggyback, Ki stumbled out into the corridor and lurched at a stoop down to the last room, fighting for breath and balance till he gained the broken window. Shuffling awkwardly, clasping the girl with one arm, he maneuvered onto the sill in a sitting position, legs dangling down the wall. Then, grabbing the rope with both hands, he moved off the ledge. Dimly he heard the voice of the old waddie above the roar of the blaze:

"The rope's scorchin'! She'll part any minute!"

Ki realized their danger. Flames were licking around, biting crisply at their feet and legs. The rope felt like a red-hot wire, and he could smell it burning. He almost lost his hold and plunged them into the fire when he grasped a spot that was already smoldering. But hand over hand, he slowly passed out of reach of the flames. The ground was still a long way off, though, and to fall now meant broken bones, or possibly death, for him and his helpless burden. His muscles were trembling, and his arms were aching from the strain that threatened to tear his hands free as he continued descending.

When he felt the rope slacken, he was still some twenty feet above the ground. Down they sailed, Ki still gripping the burned-through rope. He managed to land on his feet, with his knees bent to minimize the shock. It was severe, however, and compounded by Violet, who dropped like a millstone against him, sledgehammering him flat to the ground. For a moment everything went black before his eyes. Then he felt the strangling arms of the unconscious girl plucked from around his neck, the heavy drag of her body lifted from his back. Hands propped him upright, and someone pressed a dipper of water to his lips. As his head began to clear Ki recognized the person as Jessie.

"Thank heavens," she said fervently. "Are you okay?"

"Ask me later—like tomorrow," he croaked. Gingerly he straightened to his feet, still a mite woozy, wincing at the pain when he breathed deeply. After he prodded about his sore chest and checked here and there, he decided some ligaments and tendons might be sprained, but no ribs or bones seemed cracked or broken. Then he and Jessie went over to where Violet lay on the ground, the oldster tenderly swabbing her face with a damp rag.

Ki asked, "How is she?"

"Perkin' to." The oldster nodded, grinning. "Yup, awake and alive any moment—to your credit, I reckon. Me'n Miz Starbuck got to talkin', an' I un'erstand you go by the whittled-down handle o' Ki. I'm Rapskallion Pete Mannheim, or jus' Rap for short. Proud to meetcha."

And proud to talk, as Ki soon heard. While ministering to Violet, the garrulous Rapskallion Pete rambled on about his many years on the Rocking-G—until, moments later, he let out a cheer when Violet fluttered open her eyes.

After a short spell of coughing and gulping in air, Violet sat up, head in her hands, looking frail and sounding frailer. "Last I remember is springing for

117

the window in smoke thick enough to've cut it with a knife."

Rap told of how Ki had gone in and got her, declaring, "That was the goldurndest, slickest shovel-work I e'er seed."

"I dunno," Ki replied, shrugging. "Figured I had to get to the window somehow, and I haven't sprouted wings yet."

Violet beamed at him. "Nor have I, thanks to you."

"I'm afraid your uncle Red may've earned his pair. He wasn't in his room. Much of the floor wasn't, either. Clothes were on a chair, boots by the bed, hat and gunbelt on a post. Going by that and the look of the bed, he jumped up and fell through the hole in the floor before he could get dressed."

"He always hung his gun and hat on the bedpost," Violet murmured soberly. "I guess that's what must've happened, Ki. I guess he's gone."

"No guessin' who's to blame," Rap grumbled, staring dazedly at the fire. "Twaz that unknowed killer's gang what torched the house, and killed pore Curly, Moe, and Harry when they run outta the bunkhouse half-asleep, to see about the fire." Rap's voice had risen to a shrill. "They come bustin' in here, a whole passel of 'em on horseback, settin' fire and shootin' down folks. They'd have got me, too, if I hadn't dozed off in the outhouse. By the time I rousted and got m'self together, them demons had done their damndest—*yeow!*" Rap shouted, jumping as a crackle of shots sounded inside the burning ranch house.

"Easy, Rap," Ki said, laying a calming hand on his shoulder. "The fire's gotten to Red Greene's gun on the bedpost. That was the cartridges going off from the heat, is all."

118

Red wiped his damp brow with the back of his hand. "Thought for a minute that gang was comin' back to finish us off," he quavered. "It'd be like 'em to do that." He jerked, startled again, as the barn roof collapsed with a deafening crash, then added philosophically, "Wal, one lucky thing. All the hosses the boys didn't use were outta the barn, o'er in the field past the grove."

"And there's plenty of sleeping room in the bunkhouse," Violet noted, regarding her flame-ravaged home. "As long as the mess hall and cookshack don't catch, we shouldn't run short of food, either. Actually, I've roughed it plenty worse than this, just going out camping with Uncle Red."

Despite her optimistic words, Violet remained melancholy. She shed more than a few tears, in fact, as they placed the three murdered crewmen in a shed and covered their half-clothed bodies with blankets. Rapskallion Pete took her into the bunkhouse to scrounge up some clothing, while Jessie and Ki tended to their horses, pasturing them with the ranch stock in the field past the grove. By the time they returned, the ranch house as well as the barn were burned down to skeletons of blazing beams and timbers. For a while longer, though, they continued to keep a sharp watch on the roofs of the outbuildings, on the chance that a stray brand might ignite them.

"I imagine that's all that can be done here for now," Violet announced at length. "I'm going to have to go into Spots, I suppose. Deputy Winters will have to be told. Whenever I get back—the ashes will've likely cooled by then—I can see if we can find Uncle Red's remains for a funeral."

"We'll join you," Jessie said.

Somewhat reluctantly, Rap agreed to stay behind and

watch over the ruined ranchstead. By the time Violet had saddled up a cowpony and was riding out toward the trail, accompanied by Jessie and Ki, the once blazing flames had burned out, and the ranch house and barn were reduced to radiant heaps of fuming, guttering coals and embers.

Morning was in full glory, promising a clear and wispy-clouded day, as the three riders followed the wagon trail southerly in the direction of Ainsworth's and Lutz's spreads and, eventually, the intersection with the main road to Spots. Violet paid little heed to her surroundings, being familiar with the route and preoccupied with grief. Jessie and Ki, being cautious creatures, continually scrutinized the trail ahead, behind, and along both sides; they were all too aware that Rapskallion Pete had been right when he'd worried about the return of the outlaw band. It was clear after a night of experiencing violent, unexpected death and destruction that this killer crew was capable of anything, anywhere, anytime.

Indeed, pausing at the crest of a knoll to survey their back trail, they saw a faint smudge lying on the road behind them—a thin feather of dust lifting into the morning sky indicating a wagon or riders coming up behind them. Even as they watched, they saw a couple of black specks top the skyline a mile in back and vanish into a depression thick with pine, then moments later emerge into the open again and cross a meadow.

Ki's mouth drew into a taut line. "Are we being followed?"

Jessie shrugged. "Perhaps. Or perhaps they're angling to cut us off someplace ahead." She leaned forward to loosen her carbine in its saddle scabbard, vitally aware that she lived under the shadow of bushwhack death. After all, the mysterious murderer had visited her bedroom in the hotel to warn her that peril dogged her every step—and what with all that had occurred so far, she took that threat dead seriously.

They continued on along the wagon trail as it curved among knobs and low knolls and dipped in amongst stands of conifer and deciduous trees. As best Jessie could reckon, they were still some miles north of Ainsworth's Crosshatch and the late John Lutz's Lazy Ladder ranches. She and Ki rode with weapons ready, keeping eyes vigilant on the skyline ahead and behind them; for as the long, brush-choked grove ended and they began crossing a stretch of open country, they knew they were prime targets for ambuscade. Nothing occurred, however, and when presently they spotted the thick, first-growth forest ahead—in which lay the turn-offs to Ainsworth's and Lutz's spreads—they spurred into a gallop in a rambunctious desire to reach cover as quickly as possible. Violet, with a laugh, also urged her own mount into a quickening gait.

Their horses' swift pace probably saved their lives in the next split instant.

Somewhere behind them the stillness of the morning was shattered by the blast of a rifle. Simultaneously, something like a hot iron grazed the egg of muscle on Jessie's left shoulder.

Even as the clap of gunshot hit her eardrums, she kicked cowboots from oxbow stirrups and, clasping her carbine tightly, pitched headlong to the ground, as if the bullet had struck her squarely in the back and knocked her from the saddle. She landed in a patch of hardpan, rolled over, and lay motionless on her stomach, facing the direction of the ambush, still gripping her carbine with her finger curled around its trigger. Her sorrel mare galloped a dozen yards down the trail before halting, whinnying alarm.

"Jessie!" Violet cried, reining in and dismounting in a panic. But before the girl could reach her, Ki was out of his saddle and had hold of Violet, dragging her to cover in the underbrush flanking the trail. "She's unhurt," Ki whispered to Violet as he hunkered motionless with her. "Stay down, stay quiet. I saw Jessie, and believe me, she's okay. She's playing 'possom." Obeying, Violet abruptly relaxed and nestled in Ki's protective embrace.

A heavy silence descended. A warm gush of blood seeped down Jessie's forearm, staining her shirt, and though the bullet burn stung like a fresh brand, she forced herself to lie motionless, controlling the rise and fall of her lungs with supreme effort.

The rifle cracked a second time. Chips of stone flew up from the roadbed, showering Jessie, but now she was sure of the ambusher's location—a rocky bank along the north and west of them. Still frozen in place, she hissed across at Ki, "Well?"

"Well, it's to be a stalking game," Ki whispered back, one arm around Violet. "Whoever's firing will keep on till he hits you—or we get him."

"Well, *do* something!"

Cautioning Violet to stay put, Ki began working his way toward the slope, darting from brush to boulder, keeping as much as possible behind cover. In the silence the least noise carried. Ki thought he heard a boot scrape rock, and tensed. But it was Jessie who first reacted to the figure as it dipped stealthily out of concealment and started toward a new position. The man never lived to reach it. Jessie, rearing, triggered her carbine, and the figure stiffened and sprawled out in the rocks.

Ki then caught a muttered curse that did not come

from the man Jessie had shot. "There's another one still hiding up there," he warned Jessie and Violet in a low, urgent tone. "Stay put and cover me. I'll see if I can't prod him into showing."

Scooting over to join Violet in the covering brush, Jessie waited and watched while Ki eased slowly to higher ground. The ambusher fired, his bullet answered by two fast slugs from Jessie. Ki faulted a line of low boulders and began dashing up the slope, climbing unconcealed while the ambusher's attention was focused on the two women in the brush. More shots were traded, and a haze of powdersmoke rose from the ambusher's bouldered vantage up the slope and the two women's leafy cover below. Racing higher, at an angle, Ki approached the spot from above, on the ambusher's blind side, and was almost there when the firing ceased. Perhaps the gunman was reloading, perhaps one of them was hit.

Ki flattened, forcing himself to go slowly and very gently, so as not to be heard now that everything had fallen so quiet again. Once more he caught the sound of boots scraping against the rocks. Once more he tensed, listening, realizing the second ambusher was creeping closer, as though moving to a different vantage. The man was definitely trying to act like a snake, slithering and slouching behind rocks; but he was nervous, edgy, not always placing his hard leather boots as quietly as he should.

In such a situation it was understandable for men to grow anxious and twitchy. But Ki grew merely more icy and calculating. He was hunting a vicious sniper, but purposely employed the same cunning and techniques he would use stalking a savage four-legged mankiller. Noiselessly he inched forward, his nimble fingers feeling the razorlike *shuriken* blades that were tucked in his vest pockets. He heard a soft grunt and, aiming for it, listened for more sounds to home in on, until finally he eased into position and stared over, downward.

Below was a pock-faced man in grubby range duds. He was behind the low rockery of a small ledge, crouching on one knee while sighting a Remington rifle, tensing, prepared to blast whoever came into view.

Rising, Ki ordered, "Lay it down."

The man pivoted, firing.

Ki nailed him in the heart and throat.

The ambusher toppled awry, with his leg bent under him, his rifle still gripped in one hand, the points of two *shuriken* protruding from his chest and neck. Ki paused, ready to hurl another *shuriken* if need be. A noise behind him made him spin around, but it was only Jessie and Violet—Jessie with her pistol held ready, Violet with relief welling in her eyes.

"Thank God," Violet sighed tremulously. "Is he . . .?"

"Not yet. But I'm fairly sure he's the last."

Jessie, keeping her pistol trained, walked forward and stood over the prostrate, dying figure. "Who are you?" she demanded. "Who's your partner? Who sent you to drygulch us?"

"Don't make no difference now . . ." The man choked, grimacing with pain. "You got him, and I'm slippin' fast. The devil with you . . ."

"Who's your boss?" she urged. "Who's behind it? You'll feel better if you get it off your conscience."

"The devil with me . . ." The man shuddered, his chest heaved once, and he expired, twitching a final faint tattoo on the stony earth.

"Hell!" Disgusted, Jessie turned away.

Ki inspected the dead man's Remington, but it was a

stock "Black Hills" model .45-60 rifle, without oddities or markings that might provide clues. Then he, Jessie, and Violet clambered over the rocks to the first hombre, who was equally a stranger. His rifle was equally standard. From there they scouted for horses, which, when they were found, proved to have blotted brands and saddlebags full of standard items lacking identification. The best that could be concluded was that both men were common gun-thugs, as unwashed and nondescript as their belongings.

Except for one item. In the second gunman's shirt pocket was a square piece of paper on which was printed:

> THE FAMOUS STARBUCKERS DIDN'T GET
> OUT OF TOWN FAST ENOUGH, SO
> THEY DREW THIS BOOT HILL TICKET

"This was one printing job that was wasted," Jessie remarked coldly, tucking the grisly souvenir in a pocket. "The idea must've been to leave this card on our dead carcasses, I imagine." She glanced southeasterly, in the general direction of Spots. "In a short while, there'll be a killer who'll know he failed. But I've got a terrible premonition that this one lives by the motto *If at first you don't succeed, try, try again.*"

★

Chapter 9

Without further mishap they pushed on well into midmorning. The sky began growing unstable, either broiling in clear sunlight or chilled under gray, shifting clouds. It happened to be sunny when they reached Spots. Riding down the main street, they were somewhat surprised to find that Lester Chance, owner of the Gilded Lily, had been busy posting signs on every wall and fence post in town. The signs, apparently printed on the *Weekly Gazette Press*, offered a standing reward of five thousand dollars for the capture and conviction of Sheriff Hullinger's murderer.

"Las' Chance shouldn't have done that," Violet commented. "He'll draw the killer's vengeance before the week is out."

They reined in by the sheriff's office. Next door, in front of the locksmith shop, Thurlow Bunce was seated on a bench underneath a sign fashioned like a giant key. The blind locksmith turned his black spectacles toward the three as they dismounted and wrapped reins around the hitchpole.

"Miz Violet? Miz Starbuck? Ki?" he inquired. Then,

sensing their surprise, Bunce laughed softly as he stood up and leaned on his white cane. "You wonder how I knew who y'all was? When a gent loses the use of his eyes, his other senses get keened. I got a memory for footsteps, spur jingles—they all sing a different tune to a blind man."

Clearly bored and curious, Bunce trailed the three into the sheriff's office. Deputy Winters was sitting at the desk, hunched over a pad of paper, laboriously writing with a stubby pencil. He glanced up, appearing exasperated by his writing and relieved by the interruption. "Dag-nabit! It's beyond me how Sheriff Ike ever got his reports writ. I'd druther face a gang of bloodthirsty owlhoots! Which ain't to say I ain't. Yesterday another remuda got lifted, this time from the Currycomb outfit fresh up from Wyoming. This's horsethief heaven shore enough. Stolen animals are comin' and goin' from every whichway." Winded from his tirade, Winters took a long sigh and then asked, "What brings you folks by?"

Violet Greene recounted the tragic events.

"I's sorry, Miz Violet, abominable sorry," Winters intoned somberly when she was done. "Well, I reckon I hafta ride out with you to the Rockin'-G an' see if we can't recover your uncle, whatever's left o' him. Then I'll have Zonneveld hold an inquest, and gawd help me write another report. Dunno what this country's comin' to," he added querulously, then turned to Jessie. "If'n I heard Miz Violet rightly, you an' Ki arrived in the nick o' time early this dawnin'. An' Egg Ainsworth rode in yesterday, reportin' the raid on his place and you two bein' there on hand to help. If'n you don't mind my pryin', I thought you was goin' straight to the Greenes when you left town the tuther day. What happened?"

In terse sentences Jessie gave a brief account of their

128

stopover at Ainsworth's Crosshatch, then of tracking the raiders northwesterly onto MacLoyds' Shamrock Tail range, the rustling of their herd, and its subsequent recovery at Hoss Thief Crossin'.

The deputy's face became thoughtful. "I'm glad to be knowin' about last night's wide-loopin', and I sure wish Lorne MacLoyd had dropped by to tell me on his way to fetchin' Doc Kunkel. Y'see, when Egg Ainsworth reported his raid, he brung a hat with him, a mighty nigh new J.B. of the sort that costs considerable. He took that hat to Ferguson's general store and asked Ferguson if he could recollect selling it to anybody. Of course, Ferguson couldn't identify the hat, but he told Ainsworth that just a coupla weeks back he sold one of that sort to Bass MacLoyd. Couldn't recall selling another one to anybody recently. I reckon you know how Ainsworth came by that hat."

"Yes, I do," Jessie agreed, remembering the attempt to burn the Crosshatch buildings. "Egg Ainsworth's smart, all right. He figured something Ki and I overlooked."

Winters nodded. "Well, Ainsworth wanted to swear out a warrant charging Bass with arson and attempted murder. I arg'fied him into waiting until I talked with the MacLoyds, and seein' as how they were fightin' rustlers the very next night, it don't sound logical that Bass could be headin' up the gang. I dunno if that'll convince Ainsworth when he returns tomorrer. He can be a stubborn ol' coot."

"Have you got the hat here?" Ki asked. "Yes? May I see it?"

Winters brought the headgear and handed it to Ki. With Jessie, Ki examined it carefully. When he handed it back to the deputy, his face wore a faintly pleased expression.

"Wal?"

"Well, it's a J.B., okay."

Winters cast him an irkish look.

"I'm curious about something," Jessie said promptly. "Have you heard of anyone getting to the top of Eagle Perch?"

Winters scratched his hair. "Guess they'd have to sprout wings first. Why do you ask?"

"Because when we first rode that way yesterday, I'm sure I saw smoke rising from the top."

"Huh! Ain't that peculiar! Wal, that's a new one on me," Winters responded, shaking his head. "What about you, Thurlow? You used to drive freight all through that section and know it better'n most anyone. Ever hear tell of that?"

"Climbing to the top of Eagle Perch? Nope, never have," the blind locksmith answered. "Seein' smoke, though, that ain't too impossible to figure. Most likely it was steam, on account there're hot springs in the gorge. I reckon steam from some spring makes its way through fissures in the rock from time to time and, when the light is right, shows like smoke risin' from the top. Eagle Perch is of volcanic origin, so's the rock is basaltic and therefore plutonic, which tells the story to anyone who understands such matters."

"And just what do you mean by what you said about the rock?"

"It means, Miz Starbuck, that ages an' ages ago there was a great volcanic upheaval in this region. That column of rock was raised from the bed of the gorge to its present height by the forces at work in the depths of the earth. The formation is kinda unusual here, but years back I run acrost them in Colorado and Arizona. 'Islands in the sky' we called 'em. That is how they came to be."

"I see," Jessie said, nodding. "Easy to figure out when you understand it."

"Durned if I do," Winters complained. "Wal, if'n you're ready, Miz Violet, p'raps we'd best head down to the livery and be on our way."

As they were leaving the law office, Thurlow Bunce declared that instead of holding them up by accompanying them, he'd just go back to sitting outside his shop for a while. They paused for him to get settled, then Jessie, Ki, and Violet collected their horses and walked with Deputy Winters in the direction of the livery. They had gone about a block when Winters, glancing back to check on the blind locksmith, remarked, "Plumb smart feller, school eddicated, too, though Thurlow don't always talk like it. Every now'n then he busts loose with a flock of big words, when he gets interested in somethin' he's talkin' about. Why, I rec'lect back when he had eyes, he bought a ramshackle place outside of town and took the ol' cabin there and made it over into a fine house. It set up on a hill, and the only way to get water to it was to carry it all the way up from a spring down at the foot. Thurlow put in a contraption he called a hydraulic ram and got hisself runnin' water, no less. He couldn't keep things up after he was blinded, and had to sell. Real shame." He glanced at Violet. "Even a bigger shame about your uncle, o' course. It's a pity a decent feller like Red had to get knocked off like he did . . ."

At the livery Deputy Winters saddled a hock-scarred grulla while Violet exchanged her tuckered mount for a fresh one. Jessie and Ki, tired and seeing no reason to return to the Rocking-G, stabled their horses and, instead of joining Violet and Winters, left the livery on foot for the Ritz Palace Hotel. The deputy and the girl quickly

131

passed them, heading out of town. A few moments later Jessie had cause to wish that Deputy Winters had not left quite so soon.

The incident occurred as they were crossing the town square, angling toward the hotel. In front of the Gilded Lily Saloon, frock-coated Las' Chance was in the act of mounting a palomino gelding that was trapped out in a fancy silver-mounted saddle. Wandering his way across from Pierce's Saloon was a tipsy Osric Noonan; when the printer spotted the bar owner, he let out a caustic bellow of a laugh.

"Leavin' town, Chance?"

Swinging into stirrups, Chance acknowledged Noonan with a nod. "Heading down to Roundup," he admitted. "We're running short of stock at the Gilded Lily, and I aim to place some orders for red-eye with the jobbers there."

"Y'mean you've repented having me print that batch of reward posters for you! I wouldn't come back to Spots until the killer's scalp has been nailed up to dry."

Chance's pallid face went brick red, and he clearly struggled to control his rush of anger. "I'll be back, Osric, soon's I've transacted my business in Roundup. Meanwhile, I'd advise you to close-hobble that lip of yours."

"Meanin' what? What've I got to be close-lipped about?"

Chance picked up his reins, a thin grin playing over his lips as he stared down at the printer. "The whole town's wonderin'," he said quietly, "how come my reward posters are printed in the same style of type that the killer uses on them warning notes of his. They're wondering if you do the killer's job printing."

With an obscene oath Osric Noonan dug for the

132

Dragoon revolver holstered under the lapel of his jumper.

Before Noonan got his gun in the open, Las' Chance had flipped a .45 derringer from its spring clip under his right cuff, the deadly hideout gun leveled squarely at Noonan's chest.

Jessie gave out a gasp as she saw Ki spring across the intervening space and pounce on Noonan, felling the half-drunken printer with a chop to the jaw. Noonan's .45 landed in the dirt as the printer lay groaning on the boardwalk, a welt burning on his bruised chin.

"Thanks," Chance commented icily. He clicked the derringer out of sight under his sleeve with a deft twist of his hand. "You saved me the job of punching Noonan's ticket." Without further comment, he wheeled his palomino about and spurred off down the street, heading southward toward the county seat of Roundup.

A small crowd of punchers and townsfolk had witnessed the near shootout in front of the Gilded Lily, and clustered around as Ki lifted Noonan to his feet. From the undertaking parlor Coroner Ambrose Zonneveld strode over to where Noonan leaned against the hitching post, rubbing his sore jaw.

"I seen you draw steel against Chance, you loco fool!" Zonneveld snapped, grabbing Noonan's arm. "You ought to know better'n buck a gunslick like him. You better light a shuck over to the office and sleep off your drunk, Osric, or I'll have to locate another editor to run the *Gazette*."

Noonan shook off the coroner's grip on his sleeve and turned to snarl an oath at Ki.

Zonneveld grabbed him again. "Why should you cuss him? If he hadn't bashed you when he did, you'd be in the obituary column of the next *Gazette,* you stupid sot!"

The crowd broke up as Noonan stumbled off to his print shop and Ki rejoined Jessie. They were about to continue on to the hotel when they were hailed by Thurlow Bunce, who was groping his way along the boardwalk with his white cane.

When the blind locksmith overtook them, he asked curiously, "What was all the ruckus about?"

Jessie recounted the brief clash between Noonan and Chance.

Bunce piled gnarled hands over his cane and shook his head moodily. "This reign of terror has got to stop, Miz Starbuck, before we're all stark crazy. I got a hunch the reason Las' left town was like Osric said, 'cause he'd got a warning from the killer to vamoose. If I could only see . . ."

Jessie fell in step beside the blind locksmith as they began along the boardwalk again, Bunce shouldering his cane and linking his arm through hers for guidance. "You take your, ah, affliction very bravely," Jessie complimented. "I admire your nerve."

Bunce chuckled philosophically. "That's 'cause only five thousand dollars stands between me and regaining my eyesight. I've already had one operation in Chicago. The medicos say another operation will relieve the pressure of scar tissue against my optic nerve, and that someday I'll be able to see again."

Jessie eyed the locksmith with new interest. "I understand you were blinded by a bullet graze when bandits attacked the freighter you were driving. Surely the townsfolk here and all your old customers could pool together and loan you five thousand dollars, under the circumstances."

Bunce shook his head emphatically. "I ain't the stripe to take charity. Besides, I got an up an' comin' business

134

of my own, and it won't be too long before I've enough money saved up to make my second trip to Chicago."

They had reached the entrance to the hotel, and Thurlow Bunce fumbled in his pocket for 'makin's.' Sightless, one-handed, he rolled a cigarette, and Ki struck a match and lighted the smoke for him. With that, Bunce bid them g'day and started back to the bench in front of his shop.

Entering the hotel Jessie and Ki got keys to their rooms, where they washed up and slept off the exhausting effects of the last days and nights.

When, refreshed, they met again in the lobby, the day had lengthened into late afternoon—the dull stretch before the flurry of evening trade. The occasional local farmer or rancher moseyed by on horseback or in wagons, while on the boardwalks a few bonnetted women shopped as bored shopkeepers leaned in open doorways. Then of a sudden a drumroll of hoofbeats echoed between Spots' false fronts, and Jessie and Ki went to stare up the street in time to catch Deputy Winters, Violet Greene, and Rapskallion Pete Mannheim ride in with a string of four packhorses—one carrying a burlap sack full of Red Greene's bones, and three toting the bodies of the slain Rocking-G punchers.

Word spread like prairie wildfire. Soon the town was seething over the killing of Red Greene and his crewmen, the torching of the ranchstead, and—now a new bit of news—the running off of the Rocking-G herd. One result was a swiftly convened coroner's jury in Zonneveld's funeral parlor, where Jessie and Ki, as well as Violet and Rap, testified to a panel of locals mad as boiled hornets. Then, after a short wait, the jury members emerged from their deliberations tight-lipped and grim of face, evidently having arrived at a momentous decision.

The coroner's verdict was terse and to the point: "The four victims were killed by parties unknown. The jury recommends that Deputy Winters run them down pronto."

Deputy Winters snorted disgustedly. "Nice of 'em," he remarked in sarcastic tones. "If they hadn't mentioned it, I'd never have thought to do it."

Violet stayed after the verdict to arrange funerals for her uncle and the Rocking-G Punchers. "We'll be heading back now," she then declared, "to look after things."

"Look after what?" Zonneveld asked. "No house, no barn, no crew, no cows. . . . What's there left to lose?"

"The Rocking-G," she answered somberly.

And that was that.

By now night had once again fallen, and Jessie and Ki retired to the hotel dining room for a hearty dinner. Afterwards, Jessie remained at the hotel while Ki made a round of the two saloons to pick up any idle gossip or slips of liquor-loosened tongues.

Pierce's was having one of its habitual wild nights, but Ki quickly sensed an unusual hilarity mixed with a strange tenseness prophetic of coming events. The boisterous uproar seemed to overlay a sinister undercurrent of expectancy, of passions held strongly in leash—an ominous waiting. And as time passed and whiskey began to take effect, patrons grew truculent. Remarks were tossed back and forth between locals and trail-driving drovers, growing steadily more personal and offensive. Inevitably it led to a sudden reaching for guns.

But the heavyweight proprietor of Pierce's rose up at the end of the bar with a sawed-off shotgun in hand. "Hold it!" Pierce Demming ordered. "If there's any shootin' to be done in my joint, I'll do it. I don't aim to have no killin's in here. You bunch from the Currycomb, git goin' now till the air clears. Git now, there's 'leven buckshot in each of these ca'tridges, and I don't aim to miss."

Under the menace of the yawning twin muzzles trained upon them, the Currycomb drovers sullenly obeyed. The other patrons returned to their drinks, muttering among themselves. Demming set his shotgun down, then made his way from his chair down to where Ki was leaning against the counter.

"Understand you found Red Greene's cremated bones in the ashes."

"No," Ki replied. "That was Deputy Winters who did that, after the fire cooled down. I just happened to be there this morning when it was burning."

"Oh, yes, I stand corrected. Well, not many would take such a risk as you did, rescuing the girl an' all, and it showed mighty fast thinking, too."

Demming shook his head, sighing. "But Red, poor sinner. Red wasn't in much, but he handled his drinking and gambling real decent. I'll miss him."

When Demming walked back to his perch, Ki had the feeling he'd just been given about as close a scrutiny as he'd ever had. Despite the pleasantries, the bar owner's cold eyes had taken full measure of him—taken his measure, plucked, basted, and had him set for the oven. It made Ki think of Demming's operation here, in the adjacent trading post, and out back, and if there was some connection between the operation and the current rash of troubles.

When Ki went over to the Gilded Lily, he heard disquieting news from Deputy Winters, who was bellied up at the bar, drinking a quart of beer.

"Hell's bilin' up to Spots," Winters grumbled. "They

137

say the drovers and others who've lost livestock while trail-herdin' through here are bringin' in hired gunhands to settle scores. I heard there's a coupla dozen already on their way up from Roundup, salty hombres who know their business. They're not only ready to take any trouble that comes their way but they're out lookin' for it. There's goin' to be trouble, big trouble, sure as you're a foot high." The deputy took a large swallow of beer, wiped foam off his mouth, and continued: "I heard, too, that Estleman's Square-E and Lutz's Lazy Ladder are goin' to be sold for back taxes next month. Wonder who'll bid for 'em? Don't reckon there's over much loose money foatin' around the section right now, though. It'd be a pity if some outsider came in and took over them properties—"

"Winters!" The cry cut in from the direction of the front entrance, and turning, the deputy and Ki saw Thurlow Bunce groping his way into the saloon, waving his cane frantically as he approached the bar, his mouth was twisted in a grimace of extreme fear. "Winters! Is that fat deppity an'wheres around?" the blind locksmith bellowed when his cane rapped against the brass rail.

"Here I am!" Winters called. "What's wrong?" He reached out to grab Bunce's shoulder as Bunce groped his way in the direction of the deputy's voice.

Bunce's chest was heaving under his rapid breathing. "I think something's wrong over at the *Gazette* office," he panted. "Maybe it's a bum hunch, but I think Osric Noonan's in trouble!"

Patrons lining the bar and poker players at nearby tables crowded around Bunce and Winters, with Ki at the deputy's elbow, as Winters snapped anxiously, "What's the deal, friend?"

"It's like this," Bunce answered hoarsely. "I had to

138

go to the gen'ral store for some springs an' stuff, and on the way back, passin' the print shop, I heard a noise like a gunshot. The door was locked. I stuck my head through a window where a pane is missin' and hollered, and all the answer I got was a kind of groanin' sound. I figure Osric's in trouble!"

The saloon crowd trooped at the deputy's heels as Winters and Ki raced out into the night, gripping Thurlow Bunce's hand. Reaching the door of the *Gazette* office, Winters twisted the knob and found it locked. A ceiling lamp was burning inside the print shop, illuminating the untidy alley of type cases. Even as Winters put his face to the grimy window pane, he blurted, "I sees him!" Ki peered in, too.

The printer lay sprawled on his face at the foot of a font cabinet. Lamplight revealed a spreading pool of blood between Osric Noonan's shoulder blades.

The crowd drew back to give Winters room as the deputy drew a S&W .44 and triggered a slug at the door lock. A moment later he was kicking the door open and striding into the shadowy print shop, revolver pointing the way. Ki stalked behind the deputy as Winters crossed around the end of a paper-piled counter and knelt beside Noonan. A bullet hole was drilled into the printer's back where his suspenders crossed, the fabric of Noonan's shirt charred with gunpowder burns.

Winters holstered his revolver and, with Ki's help, rolled Noonan's inert form over on its side, then thumbed back Noonan's left eyelid. He shook his head. "Dead. The body's still warm. Reckon he bled to death inside the last five minutes."

Rising, Ki stared around. The glare of lampshine revealed a trail of smeared bloodstains across the print shop floor, coming from the direction of Noonan's printing press. "He was shot back there," Ki pointed out, "and was either dragged or managed to pull himself this far before he died. Must've been trying to reach the street door to get help, but didn't live to make it."

Bunce, leaning against the paper cutter for support, licked his lips nervously. "He was alive five minutes ago. I heard him groan!"

Winters, stepping over Noonan's corpse, followed the trail of blood down the alley of type cases, halting when he came to the rickety flatbed press. Steam was hissing in the boiler of the engine alongside the press, and a pile of newsprint, blank on the top side and printed on the other, revealed Noonan had been in the act of running off the next edition of the *Gazette* when death had struck from behind.

"Look!" Winters exclaimed, pointing toward the press. "A note!"

Ki spotted the sinister piece of paper at the same instant as the deputy. He reached out to grab the note. Printed in Condensed Gothic type was a brief, all too familiar message:

NOONAN WAS WARNED TO LEAVE
TOWN BUT WOULDN'T GO.

Deputy Winters dragged a cuff across his chalk-white face as Ki handed him the note. A stunned hush gripped the death scene as Winters read the death message aloud, and Ki walked back to where Osric Noonan lay. Kneeling down, Ki saw blood stains on an open drawer of type in the font cabinet beside the body. Evidently, Ki surmised, Noonan had managed to drag himself to the cabinet and pull open a drawer before loss of blood had finished him. Moreover, both of the dead man's hands were gripped

140

tight shut. Prying open the right hand, Ki made a strange discovery. Clutched between the fingers were four bits of type, matching the Boldface Gothic type from the opened drawer. Now Winters showed up and, along with other spectators, stared curiously as Ki inspected the four pieces of type.

One was an ampersand symbol, &. The second was a capital *H*. Another was *S*, and the last piece of type was a capital *C*.

"This'd indicate that Noonan was trying to get some type when he died," Ki commented to the deputy.

"Maybe he'd found an error in the paper he was printin'," Winters suggested, "and had stopped the press to make a correction."

"Maybe . . . although if you'll look, the typeface he was using for the newspaper is different from this type. Another thing that puzzles me is that Noonan appears to've been shot square through the spine," Ki observed, indicating the bullet wound. "A shot like that kills instantly."

"It didn't this time. It's plain enough he drug hisself from the press," Winters stated firmly. "It's also plain that whoever shot Noonan was someone he knew an' trusted. Noonan let him in—and his pal put a gun agin his back and pulled the trigger. The powder burns on his shirt prove the shot didn't come from a distance."

"If that's so, then it figures his killer stuck around only long enough to drop the note on the press, then left assuming Noonan was dead," Ki said. He took the pieces of type over to inspect them further under the glare of the ceiling lamp, moving them around as if solving a puzzle of some kind. "But why had Noonan dragged himself from the press to his type cases and picked out these three?"

"I dunno. Maybe he was trying to spell out some clue," Winters offered. "Y'know, some lead to his killer's identity."

Suddenly, like a jigsaw puzzle fitting into place, Ki believed he had divined the secret of the three bits of type. "Look here. The ampersand symbol, stands for the word 'and.' Put the letters *C* and *H* in front of it and *S* behind it, and what does it spell out?"

"*C* . . . *H* . . . an' . . . *S*," Winters drawled. "Chance!"

The hairs on Ki's neck-nape began prickling. Had Osric Noonan's last act on this side of eternity been to spell out the name of the man with whom he had nearly fought a duel a few hours before?

Winters thought so. "I heard about the near gunfray twixt Noonan an' Las' Chance while I was gone t'day. Chance supposedly left for Roundup right afterwards, but it'd been a cinch for him to double back here after dark and finish his feud. Wal, there's one quick way of findin' out if Chance is our killer." He turned to the pressing crowd. "You, Hank, and you fellows, carry Noonan over to the funeral parlor. The rest of you rubberneckers, saddle up whilst I collect some more boys for a posse. By damn, we'll be hard after Chance's arse soon's we ride. And I mean, we'll *ride!*"

Twenty minutes later the posse thundered out of Spots, Deputy Winters in the lead. Ki did not accompany them. He stood with Jessie in the hotel lobby, watching out the windows as the riders headed south under loose rein and busy spur.

Jessie sighed. "Perhaps we're wrong, Ki."

"Perhaps. If so, they'll catch up with Las' Chance before he gets very far, and just the fact he's not the hours ahead of them he should be will cook his goose."

"On the other hand, perhaps he didn't turn back, and

142

is as far ahead of them as we think."

"Then maybe we're right, and those pieces of type I found spell out *R-A-T*."

"A rat, Ki, whose rat hole lies in the opposite direction . . ."

★

Chapter 10

In the lobby of the hotel Jessie and Ki waited until midnight for the posse to return. When it did not, Jessie stretched, yawned, and said to Ki, "All right, let's play our hunch out."

Ki nodded. "All the way."

Jessie got a blank piece of paper from the hotel clerk, wrote a brief note, and paid the clerk to find a man to deliver the note to Pierce Demming at sunrise, no excuses, no questions asked. For the size of the tip the clerk readily agreed, saying he knew a drunkard who'd take the letter to Pierce's for the price of a whiskey. From the hotel they then hurried to the livery stable, where they awakened the clerk, saddled up, and rode north out of town.

By the wan light of the moon they rode as swiftly as possible along the road until they could swing off-trail and head overland to the northwest. Without rein they intersected the trail that went past the Crosshatch, the Square-E, and the Lazy Ladder, and after following it for a while, they again cut cross-country until they reached the Shamrock Tail range.

Dawn was barely a promise in the east and fog hung low over the slumbering terrain when they reined in at the MacLoyd ranchstead. The clan was already up, though, fighting a grim war to the death with huge platters of sizzling steak and eggs and pans of hot biscuits. The eggs, steaks, and biscuits were losing. The MacLoyds welcomed reinforcements, however, and Jessie and Ki were asked to get into the fight.

"No time," Jessie said, declining the invite with thanks, and she explained the reason behind their surprise visit.

The brothers raced for their weapons and horses.

Moments later, heading out, Jessie drew her mare alongside Bass's roan and asked the strapping MacLoyd, "What size hat do you wear?"

Bass scratched his head. "I got a purty big head," he replied. "I take a seven and a half."

"I imagine a seven would sort of sit up on top of your head."

"Sort of," he agreed. "Figure I'd have to spike it on to keep it from fallin' off. You need a hat? I got a new black one back at the house you can have. Wad a bunch of paper inside the sweatband and it'll fit you okay."

Jessie smiled. "No, no, I was just curious . . ."

As they neared the mouth of Eagle Perch Gorge the MacLoyd brothers split in different directions in accordance with Jessie's directions. She, Ki, and Bass continued on together along the floor of the gorge until they sighted the towering base of the Eagle Perch, its base dark and formless, its mighty crown glowing golden in the first rays of the rising sun.

Light was flooding the gorge with fire when the trio reached the base of the great pillar. They reined in and for some moments sat staring at it. Then they rode slowly around and around the formation, gazing at its

146

jagged walls that soared into the blue of the sky.

Peculiar in shape, it seemed, particularly to Jessie, that it resembled the turreted and bastioned keep of a medieval castle. The base was roughly circular and soared upward for perhaps a little over half its height to where, on the crest of the overhanging cliffs, a final rough and jagged spire shot into the sky. This spire had a slightly hollowed-out waist and an overhanging turreted effect at its crown, with a final surmounting of irregularly jutting crags. Although the base was seamed and hollowed, nowhere could be spotted a place of concealment for men and horses. Dismounting, Jessie continued her examination on foot, with Ki and Bass following her example. But to no avail; the monument was a solid mass of stone if ever Jessie had seen one. And then, when she was about to give up in disgust, her search was scantily rewarded.

Scarring a tiny patch of soft earth was a single imprint of a horse's iron, the toe pointing to the wall of stone but a few yards distant.

"Ki! Look here!"

Ki looked, squatting on his heels to carefully scrutinize the track. "It's fairly fresh," he observed, "perhaps not more than a couple of days old." He leaned back and stared at the cliff face. "Looks like the rider was heading straight for the wall, but why? It's perfectly smooth and regular."

"Well, whatever it is," Bass said irritably, "there's no sense hanging around here no longer. How about a look-see up at the gorge again, like you wanted? If our herd of cows went up it and didn't come down again, they must've corralled somewhere. P'raps there's a hole or a crack we overlooked when we was here before."

Turning their backs on the mysterious butte, the three

rode slowly up the gorge, keeping close to the east wall. Mile after mile they toiled, with the sun beating down on their backs, and discovered nothing. The line of cliffs stretched grim and unbroken, with the tangled brush growing thick and tall at their base but nowhere showing possible concealment for a herd of cows and a gang of rustlers.

Finally the dark end wall of the canyon appeared before them. It was likewise unbroken from base to lofty rimrock. With a glance at the sun, they rode across the canyon to the west wall. The cliffs on this side were more seamed and broken than those to the east, but still they could see nothing of significance. The line of growth stood stiff and unbroken but of no great depth, with nowhere any sign of a herd having been shoved through it. It might be possible, though highly improbable, that cattle could be concealed in some cleared space between the growth and the cliff face.

"Hardly a chance they could keep 'em quiet, though," Bass remarked. "Not long enough for us MacLoyds searchin' the gorge not to hear 'em. And they could never get 'em through the brush without showin' marks of their passin'."

Nevertheless, they began devoting greater attention to the wall of growth, narrowly scanning it for broken twigs or bent branches. They were perhaps a third of the way down the gorge when the appearance of the growth they were passing struck Ki as a trifle different, and he called a halt. Dismounting, he scrutinized them more closely, finding a slightly withered appearance to the leaves. When he plucked a handful of foliage, the leaves crumbled to bits under the pressure of his fingers. Then, squatting, he seized one of the stout little trunks with both hands and gave a vigorous tug.

There was no resistance of matted roots burrowing into the hard soil. Instead, the trunk slid easily from the soil, revealing its end to be a sharpened stake.

For a moment Ki held the severed trunk in his hands, showing it to Jessie and Bass. "An old trick," he said, letting it fall to the ground. He stared at the wall. "I remember we ran across something similar in Nevada not too long ago. Still, it's a good one, so long as they're careful to replace the cut bushes before the leaves begin to turn and shrivel."

"Strike me afire!" Bass exclaimed, hastily dismounting. "I ne'er seen such a bamboozle before. Well, it looks like things are beginning to clear up."

They began to pull cut bushes from the ground, making an opening in the wall of growth. For nearly a dozen feet they removed the brushy obstruction until they reached the cliff face. And in the wall of solid rock yawned a dark opening some twenty feet in width by half as much in height. In the ground before the mouth of the cave were a multitude of hoofprints, some of cattle, others of shod horses.

"Their back door out of the canyon," Jessie observed. "I imagine it leads to another gorge or canyon that gives a way onto the range and Hoss Thief Crossin' somewhere to the west."

They hesitated a moment, peering into the black mouth of the cave. Then, retracing their steps, they carefully replaced the cut bushes, and led their horses into the mouth of the cave. "Don't want anybody catchin' on just yet," Bass allowed. Remounting, they urged their horses gingerly into the shadowy opening. The light grayed quickly, the shadows deepening until they were replaced by black. The horses' hoofbeats echoed hollowly from the rocky walls and roof of the passage.

149

For a mile or more they pursued the echoing tunnel through the darkness, allowing their mounts to set the pace, confident that animal instincts would warn them of any obstruction or pitfall. They strained their own ears to catch any sound that might indicate the approach of someone from the other direction, although they had little fear of such an eventuality. Finally the shadows ahead began to gray. At last they discerned a faint spot of light, which steadily grew larger. They redoubled their caution, peering and listening.

The light grew a little stronger, although still gray and wan. A few more minutes and they passed from under the low arch of the tunnel and found themselves in a narrow draw hemmed in by cliffs even taller than those that walled Eagle Perch Gorge. The tops of the cliffs overhung, so that little light filtered down from the strip of blue sky resting on their lofty crests. For several moments the three riders sat their horses in the shadowy mouth of the cave and peered down the gloomy draw. There was no sign of movement. The silence was unbroken save for a murmur of running water somewhere ahead.

"Might as well take a chance," Bass said impatiently. "If anybody's up there, maybe we'll see them first. If we don't, well, I've a notion we won't see them at all."

As they progressed, the draw developed a more westerly trend, curving shallowly. The horses splashed through the chill waters of a little stream that weaved back and forth across the bed of the draw. For some distance the draw was little more than a slit between the soaring cliffs, then gradually it widened somewhat, though it still remained quite narrow. Clumps of brush began to appear, and groves of oak and box elder. There was evidence of the recent passage of cattle.

150

Glancing upward from time to time, Jessie arrived at a conclusion. "They could corral a herd down here without a chance of it being seen from above, even if someone happened to come prowling by."

"Yeah, and I bet that rim up there is part of the caprock," Ki added. "Chances are, it's so cut up that nobody would take a chance of riding over without a mighty good reason for doing so."

Bass grunted in agreement. "A perfect li'le hideaway, with water and enough grass growin' 'tween the bushes to keep cows goin' for a spell."

But as the draw wound on westerly they sighted no livestock, although it was clearly evident that plenty of cattle and horses had been corralled in its depths from time to time. Finally the draw narrowed again, and a little later, they reached the end, a steep and rocky slope that led up to the rimrock. It was a difficult approach, but not impossible. They picked their way to the crest, where, reined in, they gazed across the terrain to the misty hills fringing Flat Willow River.

"No question, this's their back door out of your gorge," Jessie commented to Bass. "Here's where the rustlers hole up their stolen herds and remudas till a dark rainy night comes along. Then they shove them fast along the old outlaw trail, across Hoss Thief Crossin', and to Fort Maginnis and other points north. But I don't think this's their hideout. I haven't been able to spot any sign of that."

"We will pretty soon," Ki said, "if your hunch holds up."

Bass nodded. "Uh-huh. I don't want to miss that, Jessie, so p'raps we oughta head back now."

With a glance at the sun Jessie returned with Ki and Bass down the draw and through the tunnel. They approached the entrance to Eagle Perch Gorge warily, but nothing had been disturbed. Again removing enough of the cut brush to let their horses through, they carefully replaced the bushes once more and headed along the gorge in the direction of the Eagle Perch butte.

Suddenly a bright light flared from the rimrock and flashed in Bass's face, momentarily blinding him. Squinting, he reined in sharply and, shielding his face with an arm, glanced up at the rim. "That's Doyle's signal," he declared, grinning. "Just like you ordered, Jessie, he's up there with a mirror, reflecting the word to us from my other brothers down the line. Your man's been spotted coming thisaway, just like you hunched. C'mon, let's get us'selves set!"

Galloping down the gorge, they reached the towering bulk of the butte.

"Good, everything's quiet," Jessie murmured, glancing around.

Hurriedly they concealed their horses in a dense thicket and took up positions where they could keep the trail and the butte in view.

Time passed . . .

The sun was westering when they heard the click of hoofs nearing, up the gorge. Tense and eager, they crouched in silence and watched. A few minutes later a rider loomed in the afternoon light. In range clothes and toting a Remington revolver, there, nonetheless, was no mistaking the heavyset features of Pierce Demming.

Without hesitation the saloon owner rode straight to the blank wall of the spire. At its base he dismounted, stooped, and appeared to be fumbling with something. Then he stepped back with an air of waiting. Jessie, Ki, and Bass fixed their gazes on the cliff face fronting the saloon owner; their breaths drew in sharply as they observed a dark crack appear in the gray stone near the base of the tower. The crack slowly widened, and they saw that a section of apparently solid rock was rising, doubtless into a slot prepared to receive it, and leaving an opening in the cliff face some five or six feet in width. A moment later Demming led his horse through the opening and vanished.

For tense minutes, the three crouched staring at the black square in the gray cliff face. Demming did not reappear. No sound came from the dark opening.

Ki stood up, motioned to Jessie and Bass to stay put and cover him, and circled through the brush. Afoot, he approached the opening at an angle. Hugging the cliff at the very edge of the gap, he listened intently. Then, gesturing for them to join him, he waited another moment and glided with them through the opening.

They found themselves in a rock-walled passage. With quick, light steps they stole forward. The passage, which was about ten feet in length, opened into an utterly black chamber of unknown size, the light filtering through the passage reaching only a few feet beyond its inner end. Cautiously, using their hands for guidance, they slid along the wall and stood listening, but could hear nothing.

Abruptly they realized that the light in the passage was dimming. An instant later it vanished altogether. The ponderous stone door had closed as silently as it had opened.

"Wal, we're in here but good," Bass whispered grimly, "an' if somebody don't show us the way out, we're liable to stay."

Suddenly they heard a sound, at no great distance from them, a metallic, grinding sound that they quickly interpreted as a horse pawing the stone floor with its iron.

They listened a moment longer, then Ki decided to take a chance, and fumbling a match from his vest pocket, he struck a light. Flaring up, the tiny flame revealed that they were in a rock-walled chamber, some twenty feet square with a flight of broad stone steps at the far end rising into the gloom. Other than themselves and Demming's horse, which was tethered to a peg driven into the stone, the chamber was empty. Of Demming nothing was to be seen.

Copying Ki, Bass lit a match just as Ki had to extinguish his. By the new light they navigated across to the stone steps, where the match burned out. They stood listening, but no sound came from the darkness above, so they began mounting the steps, which wound up and up through the dark. The well in which the stair ascended was not a natural formation; it had been hewn with inconceivable labor in the heart of the rock. Up and up wound the stair. It was like climbing a church steeple, or rather several steeples piled one on top of the other. The number of steps seemed endless. Soon Jessie and Bass were gasping in the stagnant air of the well, and Ki began to have an uncanny feeling that he was walking a treadmill and getting nowhere.

And then, when they had begun to despair of ever reaching the end of the appalling climb, they saw light above, a wan glow that seeped into the circular stairwell. They slowed their pace but continued to climb until they reached the final step and found themselves in another passage, which ascended for a dozen feet or so to what was apparently the open air. Over their heads hung a dense mass of rock, seamed and cracked and shattered.

With Ki in the lead, and Jessie and Bass a pace behind with pistols drawn, they crept warily along the passage, the light growing stronger as they advanced. They were almost to the end of the passage when a massive form loomed before them. There was a yelp of alarm. Ki leaped forward and caught Pierce Demming's wrist as the saloon owner's hand streaked to his revolver. Out of the passage they reeled, Demming shouting and cursing, Ki in grim silence, so interlocked that Jessie and Bass couldn't shoot at Demming without risking hitting Ki.

Struggling, the two men wrestled out across a ledge—the lofty crest of Eagle Perch butte. Ahead, the uneven surface stretched for some feet before ending at a notched and broken rim, with sunlight flooding across it. Behind, the rimrock extended upward to form a cliff perhaps twice a score of feet in height, and hollowed out of the mass of the rock was the shallow, open-fronted area on which they fought to the death.

Demming was a big man, not so tall as Ki, but heavier, and he seemed to be made of steel wires. He tore his wrist from Ki's grasp and brought his revolver around to trigger point-blank. Ki ducked, using an elbow thrust to shift both Demming and himself at angles, and the revolver thundered next to his face. He felt the shock wave of its exploding gunpowder and the snap of the bullet as it passed his ear. And then he had hold of Demming, his momentum shoving the man backwards, his left hand slashing downward in a disarming chop.

They were now at the rim—a narrow and slippery lip. And Demming, feeling himself slip, didn't fight back in any accustomed style. He grabbed Ki in a frenzied panic to balance himself, clawing with fingernails and kicking frantically.

Ki found himself battling less a man than a mauling animal. Sinewy fingers of one hand scratched and pummeled his head and torso, while Demming's other hand smashed at him with his pistol, battering his neck and upper back. He tried to swing Demming away, but the man only panicked more, grasped Ki's throat with as many fingers as he could manage and clung for dear life, strangling Ki in the process.

Ki felt one of his feet sliding off the edge. He wavered, having to compensate for himself and the man who was glued to him. He regained his foothold and tore his throat free of Demming's throttling squeeze, then jackknifed his body forward, his shoulder striking Demming midway between his ankles and knees. Demming hinged, folding over him like a bag of feed, and before the crazed man could recover and latch onto him again, Ki rolled away and stopped at the very brink of the rim. Demming vaulted over him, and a wailing cry of terror echoed through the gorge, receding hollowly down in the shadowed depths of the gorge. The scream cut off abruptly as he struck the hardpan bottom near the base of the towering butte.

Gasping, Ki rose and wavered unsteadily, daubing the sweat off his face with the sleeve of his shirt, and turned to Jessie and Bass, who were hastening across from the passage. "I wish I'd been able to take him alive," he said.

"I know," Jessie replied grimly. "For the second time in as many days we've had someone with answers slip from us—this time literally." She gazed around thoughtfully. "Old, almighty old."

"Y'mean these steps and stuff?" Bass queried. "P'raps the innards of the butte were hollowed out thisaway by ol' Indian shamans. For ceremonies like the Sun Dances I heard tell about."

Jessie shook her head. "I'm not so sure. From what I understand, tribes assemble at the beginning of summer to put on the Sun Dance to ensure good hunting and

156

general welfare, and not many tribes could all fit up here. I wouldn't be surprised if this predates the tribes now living in Montana, and was built and used simply as a watchtower in times of war or for spotting game, and—"

Her assessment was interrupted by a soft scuffing sound behind them. They pivoted around just in time to see a stubble-bearded man in scruffy clothes stepping from the mouth of the passage. He saw them, gave a bellow of alarm, and drew his pistol, firing wildly. He saw the three spring three different directions in flat sailing dives, saw his bullets spraying grit and rock shards on them and then ricocheting off. He saw his tattoo of lead hone in on the Oriental, who was the closest of the three. And the last thing the man saw was Ki suddenly rearing up and whipping his arm forward in a flickering motion. There was a brief flash in the air, as of sun glinting on shining metal—

And Ki's *shuriken* buried itself in the bridge of the gunman's nose, several of its razor points penetrating into the frontal lobe of his brain.

The gunman did a strange little dance, a one-legged spin on his heel, as blood spurted around the edges of the *shuriken*. Then he slammed backwards into the passage.

From the passage sounded a chorus of muffled yells and curses.

Crouching low, Jessie and Bass heard the commotion inside the passage and responded by triggering a couple of bullets through the opening. There was an answering salvo of shots, forcing them to lie flat as bullets cut the air inches above them. The firing tapered off, but not because the gunmen were giving up. No, it was just that it was as clear to them as to the three on the rim that the gunfray was a standoff for the time being—a stalemate

157

in which the gunmen couldn't show themselves without getting hit, and the three couldn't do anything but lie flat for the same reason.

"Just what," Bass hissed at Jessie, "was in your note?"

"Believe me, I didn't invite the whole blessed gang," she retorted. "I merely wrote Demming, saying 'Trouble. Come at once.'"

"Well, you're right, Jessie, there's trouble here," Ki said. "Bass, let's hope your brothers hear the ruckus and come at once. We can hold this bunch off till we're out of ammunition or light, whichever's first, but as soon as it's nightfall . . ." He made a slicing gesture with his thumb across his throat, rising just enough to do so to set off another fusillade of gunfire.

In response, Jessie and Bass again poured slugs at what they thought was movement just inside the passage. They hardly heard the report of their own guns. It was drowned by a shattering roar that continued in a series of muffled thunderclaps through which knifed faintly a wild scream of agony and terror. From the mouth of the passage boiled a cloud of dust. For a moment they stared in bewilderment.

Then the explanation rushed to Jessie. "My God! The vibrations set up by their gunfire loosened that cracked roof in the passage and brought it down on top of them!"

Her flesh crawled as she envisioned the awful fate of the rustling gang, crushed and mangled under tons of stone, some perhaps dying slowly in blood and agony in the dark. She stood up stiffly, followed by Bass and Ki, and together they stared at the settling dust cloud. Wiping the cold sweat from her face, Jessie walked to the broken rim and stared into the depths of the gorge. A moment later she glimpsed a man driving a horse madly up the canyon.

"The boss, the real chief of this gang, is getting away," she reported. "I guess he must've been on the outside when the roof caved in."

Face bleak, eyes cold, she watched until the fleeing figure had vanished amid the growth and shadows. Then, to her surprise, she spotted the other MacLoyd boys galloping toward the butte from down the gorge. There was no way to signal them to ride on past the butte and pursue the outlaw leader before he could escape through the tunnel and draw—no way to signal anything except that they were up atop the butte, which Bass did straightaway with a gunshot. His brothers reined in around the butte, shouting and gesturing upwards. Bass yelled and gestured in return.

But he might as well have saved his energy, Jessie realized glumly. The roof of the passage, falling in, had sealed any chance of their return, leaving them in a worse predicament than before, marooned atop the great butte without food or water. The chance of the MacLoyd brothers rescuing them was equally nil. No human ingenuity could bridge the space between them and the gorge floor. No, they were absolutely on their own. If anything could be done, it was up to them to do it.

However, when she consulted with Ki and Bass, they quickly arrived at a decision. Better a swift and merciful death on the rocks below than a lingering one from thirst and starvation. After Bass tightened his belt and waved a final time to his kin far below, they lowered themselves over the dizzy rimrock and began the hazardous descent.

The task was not so difficult as it appeared from above. Handholds were plentiful, and the broader ledges gave them a chance to rest a little from time to time. But it was bad enough. Their hands were soon torn and bloodied, their clothing rent by the sharp angles of the stones. Very quickly they were drenched with sweat and gasping for breath. Once they were forced to slide down the almost perpendicular slant for nearly a dozen feet, with no guarantee that they would come to rest on the narrow ledge for which they were sliding.

Finally, when their stretch was all but exhausted, they reached the broad platform at the base of the upper spire. There they lay resting for some time, Bass conversing in shouts with his brothers, before they attempted the last half of the descent.

The final downward climb was less difficult than the upper spire, but to Jessie, dizzy with fatigue and aching in every muscle, it seemed endless. It was with a surge of heartfelt relief that she felt her feet touch the solid ground she had never hoped to reach alive.

She rested again, along with Ki and Bass, his brothers crowding around with endless exclamations and questions. Then Jessie and Ki left the MacLoyds and walked around the pillar to where Pierce Demming lay asprawl, and if it hadn't been for the seepage of blood from the bar owner's nose, mouth, and ears, it would have appeared he was sleeping peacefully in the shadow of the butte. From Demming they went over to try and discover the secret of the mysterious rising door. Shortly, they had to give it up. The face of the rock was webbed with cracks, and it was impossible to ascertain the exact location of the stone panel. The chances were, too, that the mechanism which operated it had been smashed and jammed by the avalanche of broken rock pouring down the well. The mechanism was doubtless quite simple, the door being moved on some familiar balance principle. Some simple lever, moved ever so little by pressure on a secret spot, no doubt threw additional weight on a hidden counterbalance and caused the huge mass to be lifted from the ground, where it remained suspended until the weight slowly shifted back by its own accord and allowed the massive panel to descend once more.

Returning to the MacLoyds, Jessie said, "It's more than likely a lost cause, but you fellows know the terrain, and you, Bass, know the tunnel. Head on out after the gang's boss, and perhaps you'll run him down or run across him out there somewheres."

"And you, Jessie?" Bass asked.

"We're heading back to town. I'm betting that's where the boss will wind up, if you don't get him first."

Retrieving their patiently waiting horses from the thicket, Jessie and Ki mounted and rode down the canyon, eager to press forward with gathering speed.

★

Chapter 11

Indigo twilight had given way to star-spangled nightfall by the time Jessie and Ki arrived back in Spots. They had stabled their tuckered mounts at the livery and were walking to the hotel when Deputy Winters hailed them from the door of the sheriff's office.

"Sure glad to see y'all back in one piece," Winters said when they came up to him. "Me 'n' my posse rode most all last night and caught nary a sign of Las' Chance, so we didn't know who else he may've kilt. He escaped us like he'd vanished into thin air."

"Either that, or Las' Chance was far ahead on his way to Roundup, just like he said," Jessie replied. "If he returns to town in a few days with an order for whiskey, you'll know you've been chasing the wrong man. Right now, I'm pretty sure you were."

"Izzat so? Why?"

"Because of where we've been. The Shamrock Tail."

"A-hah! Them MacLoyds are behind all this! I knew it, I knew it all along. That hat Ainsworth thought belonged to Bass MacLoyd is the clincher!"

"Calm down, Deputy. Egg Ainsworth's a smart oldster,

but he sort of jumped at conclusions. The hat you showed us was a size seven. Bass happens to take a seven and a half. That hat would have had to've been pinned on his head, and I don't think he ever used a hatpin. No, what I'm referring to is what Bass and his brothers helped us track down—the secret to all the rustling and raiding." Jessie then recounted their discoveries in Eagle Perch Gorge and the subsequent fight up in the butte, ending with the deaths of Pierce Demming and his gang. "Demming was the chief of the livestock-thieving band that's been riding high, wide, and handsome around here. As a bar owner, he was positioned perfectly to learn when trail drives were coming through. And as trading post owner, he was selling stolen horses back to his victims. Of course, most of the remudas were choused on to Fort Maginnis, which has been buying great numbers of mounts for the cavalry troops engaged in the current Indian campaign. The fort is where he sold most of the rustled cattle, too."

Deputy Winters listened intently, his eyes bulging as he heard of Pierce Demming's activities. "We had the wool pulled over our eyes for fair!" he declared. "Why, Demming was the worst varmint in Montana!"

"Correction—*second* worst. Demming was giving orders, true, but he also must've been taking orders from someone else. Demming had a good deal going here; he had no reason to kill off ranch owners or Noonan or Sheriff Hullinger, much less leave death threat notes." Frowning, Jessie shook her head. "No, what's been happening only makes sense if there's someone else involved, someone with another, darker motive."

"Wal, who is it?"

"That's what I'm betting on learning tonight." Jessie

went on to explain about the warning on the lantern glass and showed the deputy the note taken from the dead ambusher. "I'm now a double threat to the killer. He's failed to kill me, and since he operates using fear tactics, he can't afford failure. Also, with our breakup of Demming and his gang he knows I'm onto him, and he's got to get me out of the way fast. Tonight I'll be in my hotel room, and I'm betting he'll try to strike then, if given a chance."

"I'll make damn sure he won't get no chance!" Winters bellowed. "I'll organize a sort of posse to protect the hotel. I'll—"

"Thanks for staking a night's sleep in my behalf," Jessie cut in, "but he'll just try some other time. It's better if Ki and I bait a trap for him. We'll need three buckets of paint to do the job."

The deputy looked fit to explode. "If Sheriff Ike was alive, he wouldn't let you go through with any such crazy notions, Miz Starbuck! How you aim to trap anybody with paint?"

"That," Jessie said tantalizingly, "remains to be seen . . ."

Heading on to the Ritz Palace, Jessie and Ki picked up their keys and ascended the stairs. The corridor leading to their rooms could only be reached by the stairs; no other exit opened off the long hallway—a fact that they took into careful consideration. If the killer sought to attack Jessie in her room tonight, his only way to reach her would be through the downstairs lobby and along the dark corridor.

Entering Jessie's room, they glanced around to confirm their memories. There was no attic in the hotel. No stalking murderer could crawl over and shoot her through the ceiling of her room. Indeed, the ceiling was built on a slope, with a series of steeply-pitched rafters covered with weather-beaten shingles. And the room had but one window. Going to it, Ki ran up the sash, and they peered outside.

Ten feet away was the unpainted wall of the abandoned Sparks Grand National Opera House, its swaybacked roof showing bald spots where time and the elements had ripped off patches of shingles. On the level with her window were a series of windows marking backstage dressing rooms of the opera house. At least three of them would give a drygulcher a view across into her hotel room.

"The only possible way the killer could draw a bead on me would be from one of those dressing room windows," Jessie remarked to Ki. "It isn't likely he'd risk coming up the hallway from the public lobby."

"Let's hope you're right. It's the only way the paint trick has any hope of flushing out our man."

"Which reminds me, Ki. We'd best get that paint before Mr. Ferguson closes Ferguson's General Store."

Going back out to the main street, they walked a couple of blocks and found the store still open. Ferguson was preparing to lock up for the night, however, hauling in his displays hanging over the boardwalk and lining his window-front tables. Jessie asked him if he sold paint by the gallon.

The pudding-faced storekeeper nodded. "What color?"

"Bright."

He regarded Jessie as though she were addled. "Bright what?"

"Whatever you've got. The brightest."

"Well, I got a dozen gallon-buckets of wagon yaller."

"Fine. We'll take three."

Scratching his bald spot, Ferguson went into the rear of

the store and carried out three buckets, one by one. Jessie paid him, and Ki carried the buckets out to the boardwalk, where out of earshot of the storekeeper Jessie told him, "I'll go over to the livery and get our lass'-ropes. You sure you don't want me to help?"

"No, this'll be a piece of cake." Balancing the buckets by looping his arm through bails so as to keep one hand free for emergencies, Ki angled around back of the store and worked his way across weed-filled back lots until he was behind the Ritz Palace Hotel. From there he headed for the adjacent Grand National Opera House, moving with infinite stealth to avoid stepping on the tin cans and assorted junk which littered the back alley. Reaching the weather-beaten rear wall of the abandoned theater, he worked his way around into the alley between it and the hotel. Fifteen feet above him was the window of Jessie's room.

The stage door, Ki saw, hung ajar on rusted hinges. Feeling his way through the darkness, he wedged his way through the doorway without having to open it further. A faint wash of starshine coming through a skylight high overhead gave him enough light to recognize certain objects without having to open it wider. A maze of canvas props and flats were stacked against the rear wall. The stage was thick with dust and littered with debris. A moth-eaten curtain hung over the row of coal-oil footlights that extended between the tarnished gilt arches of the proscenium.

Dimly visible in the gloom was a spiral staircase leading to the dressing rooms backstage. Ki padded to the stairs and was grateful to find that they were of iron, the treads giving off no telltale squeak under his weight. Arriving at the gallery overlooking the backstage area, he groped his way along the open doors to where the jugglers, acrobats, magicians, singers, and dancers of a bygone era had once daubed on their greasepaint and changed their costumes.

Setting down his three buckets of paint, he paused in the clotted shadows, ears straining. But the cavernous auditorium beyond the stage was deserted. Wind moaned around the eaves and through the broken shingles, where stars peeped through the roof. Somewhere off in the tangle of curtain ropes beyond the gallery railing, a rat was gnawing away at a wooden timber.

Ki groped through one of the dressing room doors, seeing the square gray outline marking a window. In silhouette against the opening was the upright post of an old-fashioned bedstead; apparently Spots' theatrical troupes had slept in their dressing rooms. The window had long since lost its glass. Floorboards creaked as he leaned over the warped windowsill, seeing to his satisfaction that he was in the room directly opposite the window of Jessie's hotel room.

Going out of the dressing room, he set the buckets of paint down and pried open the lid of one bucket. Then, working by touch alone, he pulled the door of the dressing room until it was nearly shut and balanced the open bucket of paint on its upper edge, the rim of the bucket resting against the door frame for support. Any prowler who attempted to enter the dressing room would upset the paint bucket and spill its contents over himself.

With the remaining buckets of paint, Ki set similar traps on top of the doors leading into the adjoining dressing rooms, which were also opposite Jessie's hotel room. His preliminary plans completed, he went down the spiral stairway, crossed the musty-smelling backstage area, and slipped out through the alley door. He made a circuit of the Grand National Opera House, arriving at the main street facade of the theater, where he checked the front doors and found them locked.

Returning to the hotel, Ki found eight burly men, heavily armed, seated around the lobby. They eyed him narrowly as he crossed to the stairs but said nothing until he started up. Then, behind him, he overheard one of the men say loudly, "Aw'ri', boys, there goes Miz Starbuck's bodyguard. Look lively, now. Orders is nobody else goes upstairs, not till sunrise, not alive anyhow."

At the top of the stairs he noticed that the corridor was no longer dark. Lighted lanterns were hanging on alternate doorknobs down the entire length of the hall. Deputy Winters sat in a Morris chair on the landing, a double-barreled shotgun cradled across his lap, a deer rifle leaning against the wall by his chair. From his vantage point Winters had a clear view of the lighted corridor, as well as the lobby stairway.

"It's like this," Winters told Ki. "I got deputized men spendin' the night downstairs, just to make sure the killer—whoever he is—don't go upstairs. And I personally aim to squat here to make sure nobody enters or leaves the hotel."

Ki grinned thinly. "How about the other guests in the other rooms?"

Winters shook his head, scowling. "Nobody's stayin' up here tonight but you and Miz Starbuck. She's in her room, and now that you're here, p'raps you can help me talk her outta her female contrariness. Y'all oughta stay down there surrounded by me an' my men. There's safety in numbers. The killer wouldn't dare to show hisself to attack her."

"As long as she's got so many friends pulling for her,

I reckon she's plumb safe." Ki chuckled. "Good night, amigo."

Heading down the corridor, Ki rapped on Jessie's door and waited a moment before she unlocked it and let him in.

"All set?" she asked, and when Ki nodded, she indicated the two coils of lasso rope she'd brought back from their gear at the livery. "Well, we're set here about as much as we can be. Maybe more than I'd wish, with Deputy Winters and his men bruiting about. He even posted some in the alley."

Stepping to the window, Ki stood staring at the dressing room windows across the alley. Below, in the darkness, he could see the ebb and glow of cigarettes as guards conversed with each other at the two ends of the alleyway. "Well, we might as well settle in. This could be a long wait."

It was. Jessie stretched out on the rickety bed while Ki, placing a chair alongside the wall to the left of the open window, seated himself there with one of the coiled lassos in his lap. In spite of themselves, fatigue and nervous strain caused them to doze off, but they slept lightly, as hunted animals sleep, subconscious standing guard on the alert to awaken them at the slightest strange noise.

On the hour, half hour, and three-quarter mark, the courthouse clock tolled the time. The moon arced slowly across the sky and eventually slid down behind the swaybacked ridgepole of the Grand National Opera House, throwing the alley and the hotel wall into shadow. . . .

It seemed as though an eternity had passed when finally the clock struck four a.m. On the last reverberating note of the chime, as it was trembling into nothingness across the night air, a crash sounded inside one of the dressing rooms of the theater across the alley. It was followed by a dull clatter of booted feet along the resounding catwalk of the backstage gallery.

"My trick worked!" Jessie exulted, springing from the bed.

Already Ki was shaking out the loop of his lariat and moving to the window. A dozen feet away he could make out the dim outlines of the bedpost outside the dressing room opposite. With inbred skill and the training of long practice on the range, he sent his noose snaking out across the alley and into the dressing room window. The loop settled over the bedpost, a simple feat for a man who had roped countless steers from the hurricane deck of a peg pony.

Behind him Jessie hurriedly lashed the end of the lasso securely to her own bedpost. "I'm going across, Ki."

"No, you're not, Jes—"

"Yes, I am," she insisted in a tone brooking no argument. "For Ike Hullinger." With that, she straddled the windowsill and leaped out into space, her hands locking over the rope that spanned the black alley fifteen feet above the ground.

The rope sagged slightly under her weight, but held as Jessie swung her way hand-over-hand across the brief space, invisible to the eyes of the guards at either end of the alley. Her cowboots touched the clapboard wall of the opera house. A moment later she was gripping the windowsill of the dressing room and hoisting herself inside the theater. Moonlight penciling in through breaks in the roof revealed the puddle of lemon-yellow paint that covered the threshold of the dressing room and spattered the wide-open door. The killer, then, had chosen to enter the middle of the three dressing rooms opposite her hotel room window.

Pistol in hand, Jessie leaped over the pool of paint and sidestepped quickly to put herself out of the bar of moonlight slanting down from the skylight. From somewhere at the far end of the backstage gallery a gunshot blasted echoes inside the abandoned theater and a bullet slammed into the flimsy wall beside her. Dropping to a squat, she triggered, aiming at the muzzle-flash she'd glimpsed at the far end of the catwalk. A yell of desperation and rage followed the report.

For an instant Jessie believed her bullet had struck. Then she picked up the sharp rataplan of boots racing around the corner of the gallery, heading for the top of the spiral staircase. Flame spat from the darkness there, and a slug ricocheted from the iron railing in front of her. Gunsmoke blossomed in a blue-white smudge in a shaft of moonlight twenty feet away, and from behind could be heard a wild scrambling flight down the spiral stairs. Once the killer reached stage level, Jessie realized, he stood a chance to escape the opera house from any one of a number of doors or windows.

Holstering her pistol, she leaped to the top of the gallery guard railing, balancing on the iron balustrade. The backstage floor was twenty feet below, but Jessie leaped toward a taut rope used for raising and lowering the curtain. The rough braided Manila hemp burned her palms as she slid down the big rope. Her boots landed on the floor before the killer had succeeded in reaching the foot of the spiral staircase.

Dipping back into shadow, then, Jessie redrew her pistol and charged forward, aiming to block the killer's escape from the foot of the stairs. Even as she did so, she caught sight of a hurtling figure flashing past a bar of moonlight as the killer leaped headlong from the staircase. The warped floorboards of the stage trembled under the impact of the killer's landing, and simultaneously, he opened fire. With screaming lead bracketing her body, Jessie flung herself flat on the stage.

Hunter and fugitive lay there, waiting for the other to make a move, to make a mistake. For the first time Jessie became aware of the bedlam of shouts outside the theater building. The roar of gunfire inside the opera house had roused the town. Then she caught a glimpse of another figure passing over one of the pools of moonlight that mottled the stage area.

"Get down, Ki!" she called. "Get back!"

No doubt the killer perceived the predicament he was in, now aware that two people were after him inside and plenty more were surrounding him on the outside. Either panicking or figuring Jessie was momentarily diverted by Ki's sudden presence, the killer made a break for it, then, leaping to his feet and sprinting across the center of the stage, avoiding the tangle of ropes and standing scenery, steering clear of the patches of moonlight on the floor.

Jessie was in immediate pursuit. Glass jangled as the killer stumbled over a footlamp and sprawled headlong into the cobwebby gulf of the orchestra pit. As Jessie veered off to the left side of the stage and paused beside the gilded proscenium, she heard a jingle of metal down in the orchestra pit as the killer ejected spent cartridges from his revolver. She did not hear Ki closing on slippered feet and winging one of his daggers into the pit, but she did catch the metallic clatter of its blade striking against the keyboard of a piano somewhere in the darkness.

Even as the discordant notes jangled out, the killer vaulted over the low railing that separated the orchestra pit from the ghostly auditorium and opened fire at the general direction of Jessie. His bullets fell wide, Jessie already groping her way through the darkness toward a better vantage. But the gun-flame from his revolver gave her the exact location of her quarry, crouched now at the lower end of the theater's center aisle. With cold precision Jessie triggered her pistol, spacing a pattern of shots above and below and to each side of the flaming gun.

She was rewarded by a high-pitched scream of agony. At least one of her slugs had struck home. "Give it up!" she shouted, peering around the corner of the proscenium. "Toss out your gun and give up! Now!"

A choked oath, more the frenzied bawl of a wounded predator than a human sound, answered her challenge. Then, for a shaved fraction of an instant, Jessie caught sight of the killer as, wounded, he darted through a patch of moonlight, sprinting up the aisle toward the front entrance of the theater. She had a dead bead on him and triggered instantly—only to hear the click of the firing pin against a spent shell. In the wild exchange of shots she had emptied her pistol.

Reloading with desperate haste, Jessie now saw Ki make a running leap off the stage into the orchestra pit, then vault over a low velvet-draped railing onto the auditorium floor. She raced to follow, hearing ahead through the gloom the killer stumbling desperately toward the far end of the theater. Spatters of crimson where the moonlight struck the moldy carpeting of the center aisle were proof that her bullets had struck their target. But how badly the killer was wounded, she could not tell.

174

A gun roared from under the peanut-gallery balcony as the wounded killer turned to shoot at Ki as Ki sped up the aisle. The bullet thudded into a plush-covered seat a dozen feet in front of him. Then, as Ki zigzagged his way to the halfway mark up the aisle, there came the squeak of door hinges as the killer swung open the street entrance to the theater—the door that Ki had checked and found locked earlier that night. The killer, therefore, had the keys of the abandoned building in his possession and had gained entry from the front.

The gray light of approaching dawn silhouetted the killer as, crawling on hands and knees, he dragged himself over the threshold and out on the porch, which faced the main street. Like a crippled spider, he hitched around to face the interior of the theater. Through the open doorway both Jessie and Ki saw him struggling to lift his revolver for the final shootout. But even as they moved grimly forward, they saw the revolver sag in the killer's grasp.

At such close range Jessie and Ki could have easily killed the man. But they held off as the killer exhaled a long choking sigh and then wilted in an inert heap, facedown across the threshold of the theater entrance.

Ki leaped forward and snatched up the killer's smoking revolver. He stepped over the motionless form and was joined by Jessie; they stood blinking their eyes against the glare of lanterns that Winters and his deputized guards were carrying up on the theater porch behind a bristling array of guns. Crowding around, everyone stared down at the figure whose head and shoulders were dripping with yellow paint. Blood seeped from bullet holes in his chest and abdomen, grim evidence of the accuracy of Jessie's custom pistol.

175

"Here's your killer," Jessie told Deputy Winters. "Don't be surprised when we turn him over. You've all respected him as an honest member of your town."

Ki stooped to roll the killer over on his back, revealing the man's paint-spattered, blood-smeared visage for the first time.

"No, it can't be!" Winters choked. "You've made a horrid mistake!"

"I knew you'd be surprised and grieved," Jessie replied. "That's why I didn't tell you my hunch until I could back it up. Now I can, and here he is. Thurlow Bunce."

Chapter 12

Even as the crowd gaped in disbelief they saw Spots'
locksmith open the glittering eyes that had been hidden
for so long behind a blind man's dark glasses. But there
was nothing of blindness in the hate-poisoned glare that
the dying murderer shot up at Jessie and Ki, and then
Deputy Winters.

"Yeah." Crimson bubbles frothed the corners of
Bunce's mouth as Ki helped him into a sitting position,
propped up against the theater door. "No use claimin' . . .
yuh made a mistake."

Kneeling beside him, Jessie turned to glance around at
the faces of the crowd. "Is Doc Kunkel here? No? Then
somebody go fetch him."

"I doubt a medico can help," Winters said dubiously, as
one of his deputized guards hastened off in the direction
of the doctor's home. The crowd pressed closer, still
unable to believe that their reign of terror had come
to an end in the exposing of this pitiful wounded figure
they had believed to be a blind man, incapable of filling
the killer's role.

"You're wondering about Bunce's eyesight," Jessie

remarked. "If my guess is correct, the Chicago surgeons restored your sight on your first trip there, didn't they, Thurlow? You've masked the fact behind your dark glasses all these months, haven't you?"

"Y-yeah," he repeated. "Nobody knew. I figgered I . . . I could kill off the ranchers or scare 'em into sellin' out cheap with warnin's I printed up. But how . . . how'd you tumble to me?"

"You made three mistakes, Thurlow. Or at least three that finally made me catch on. The one that clinched it was when Miss Violet, Ki, and myself rode in from her ranch, and you called us all by name. Now, possibly you could've recognized Miss Violet and myself like you said you did, but Ki wears moccasin-style slippers, and he didn't say a thing, so you couldn't pretend to have recognized his voice or jingle of his spurs or heavy step. Then later that afternoon you slipped again the same way when you came hurrying up after the fight between Noonan and Las' Chance. Ki and I were just standing there, making no sound at all, yet you identified us from twenty feet away. That proved to me you weren't stone blind, as you pretended to be."

Ki saw the crowd shaking their heads, still unable to believe Jessie despite Bunce's confession. So he said to them, "Knowing Bunce isn't blind, it isn't hard to piece the puzzle together. Being an expert key maker, he had no trouble making keys that'd let him into the print shop. Working in the dead of night, he set up type and printed warnings and boasts. Being a friend and confidant of Sheriff Hullinger, he found it easy to stab the sheriff in the back while the sheriff was eating, leaving a note saying the sheriff had ignored his warning. Actually, I think Bunce killed him because Flora had asked for a Starbuck force to come help her grandfather—which the sheriff had no doubt confided to Bunce—and Bunce couldn't risk Hullinger and Starbuckers putting their heads together in an investigation."

"And Bunce found you 'n Miz Starbuck were here in answer to Flora's request," Winters interrupted, "when he snuck out into the hotel garden and eavesdropped on her conversation with Flora."

Before Ki could answer, Thurlow Bunce nodded in confirmation of the deputy's statement. "It all went wrong after that. Miz Starbuck almost trapped me in the hotel that same night, when I'd written that warnin' on her lamp chimney with a piece of beeswax. I didn't want to fire a shot and attract attention when she almost bumped into me in the dark hall, but all the same I felt lucky I didn't get kilt then 'n there."

Life was obviously ebbing rapidly from Bunce, and Jessie hastened on with the explanation, wanting for her own satisfaction to have the dying killer confirm her reconstruction of the events. "Bunce showed a certain devilish skill in throwing suspicion on others. He used type from the print shop for his notes, something that put Noonan under suspicion. Only then Noonan got suspicious and went to check through his type, so Noonan had to die. When Bunce shot him, he turned suspicion on Las' Chance by leaving type in Noonan's hand that spelled out Chance's last name."

Bunce leered up at Deputy Winters. "I was in hopes . . . you'd go off half-cocked, like yuh did, and capture Chance an' give him a vigilante trial, which yuh didn't. That would've put me in the free 'n' clear."

"But why, Thurlow? Why'd you go crooked and do all this?"

Bunce responded to the deputy's query with a fit of coughing that left him weak and gasping. Jessie answered

179

instead. "The railroad. You see, there really will be a railroad coming through this section in the next few years."

"Through Spots?" Winters blurted. "It will sure boom the place if they do."

Jessie smiled and shook her head. "Spots will probably die with her boots on, just a ghost town, nothing but a name and a legend. No, the railroad is going to pass through to the west of here—across Estleman's and Ainsworth's ranches, either the Lazy Ladder or the Crosshatch, and for sure across the Shamrock Tail, and boost land values in the process. After Ki and I got a lay of the land, I got to thinking about Bunce's comments about the railroad not coming through, and if it ever did, it'd come through Spots. He knew better. He'd been a freighter, and knew there was a sizable market hereabouts and up around Lewistown all the way to the border. A spur line would be a certitude. And well acquainted with the terrain as he was, only a slight education in engineering would tell him that the road would never pass through Spots. Too many construction difficulties are involved. But following that old outlaw trail across those spreads is a much easier grade and a straight shoot to the shallow Hoss Thief Crossin', where the Flat Willow River would be easiest to bridge. Of course, we had no reason to suspect Bunce of anything off-color—then—but his attitude tied up with other things later on."

"Y'mean like actin' blind when he could see?"

"Yes, and his deliberate lie about the smoke I saw coming from atop the butte in Eagle Perch Gorge," Jessie explained to the deputy. "If you recall, when I mentioned the smoke, he insisted it must've been steam filtering up from a hot spring. That might've passed if he hadn't

180

tried to bolster up the idea. He went on to say that the butte was basaltic and plutonic rock, indicating volcanic action. Might be true, if the rock was basaltic, but it's not. There're no striations—regular, parallel grooves or channels striping the rock—which would be the case if the butte had been formed by volcanic action. Also, it's not the right kind of rock. Bunce spoke in terms that only a man educated in geology and petrology would employ, which made his explanation of the smoke fantastic, just as his theory regarding its formation was nonsense."

"Sure sounded convincin' to me," Winters confessed. "Then how did that darn thing come to be? It looks almost like it was built by hand."

"Simple. The Eagle Perch consists of very hard and very tough rock that's much more resistant to weathering than the other formations in the gorge. Ages ago, the gorge was formed the same way as the Colorado Canyon, the Santa Helena Canyon of the Rio Grande, and others were formed—by rushing water cutting down through the softer strata of soil between walls of harder rock. The butte is a shaft of harder rock, similar to the walls of the gorge, and as the water wore away the soil to form the gorge it could make little impression on the shaft, and it was left standing. Bunce must've known that, and I knew he must've known it. He thought he was talking to a silly girl unfamiliar with geological phenomena, of course."

"And when he went to such lengths to explain away the smoke, you wondered why, eh?"

"Exactly," Jessie agreed. "I imagine someone caught hel-heck over that smoke. The top of Eagle Perch, of course, was Demming's gang's hideout. They could vanish there when pursued, and it gave them a watchtower from which they could survey the whole surrounding range."

"Twaz Demming who learnt of it," Bunce interjected, still coughing and wheezing feebly. "Somehow or t'uther . . . from an Indian or through his years as a cardsharp an' wide-looper . . . he learnt the secret of the door leadin' to the stairway, and when he moved here and we hooked up . . . he put it to use, just like he put to use that way outta the gorge . . . the only way that a herd could be sneaked out and over to the ol' Owlhoot Trail."

"Then the smoke?" Winters pressed.

"Like the lady figgers . . . One of Demming's bunch lighted a fire up there to boil coffee, or sumpthin', forgettin' the smoke would show agin the sky and be sure to arouse the curiosity of anyone chancin' to see it . . . She did, and she pursued it down to endin' that whole gang, and I . . . I knew it'd only be a matter of time afore she got onto me, if'n I didn't get her first. First an' fast . . ." Bunce shook his head slowly, wincing from the pain of his bullet-riddled body. "After I got her, I aimed to keep workin' under cover till I bought up all the properties cheap. . . . Then I'd take a trip like I was goin' for another operation and . . . come back with my eyesight, the owner o' that entire section. . . ."

"Instead the lady got you—with a gallon of paint."

Jessie had to smile despite the tragic scene. "Ki and I counted on Bunce thinking he'd have to strike quickly. As long as I stayed in my hotel room, we knew he could only get at me by shooting or tossing a black powder stick into my window. That meant he had to work from one of the old dressing rooms in the theater, so Ki set up buckets of paint to spoil his plans and identify him at the same time, in case he got out of the theater."

Thurlow Bunce groped in the pocket of his paint-soaked

182

jacket and drew out a cartridge of blasting powder to which was attached a short fuse. Tossed into Jessie's room, the bomb Bunce had improvised would have blown her, Ki, and a goodly portion of the hotel to kingdom come. "My original plan was to visit yuh in your room. I didn't think . . . you'd suspected me quite yet. A knife would've done the trick. But when I found the hotel guarded, I unlocked the opery house with keys I'd made for the front door . . . and aimed to use that stick o'—" Suddenly Bunce shuddered, closing his eyes, and wilted with a sigh as if overcome with fatigue.

Jessie cleared her throat. Ki rose to his feet, staring down at the figure of the killer.

Deputy Winters shook their hands. "The town can never thank you enough," he declared solemnly. "We'll never forget."

There was a commotion at the rear of the crowd, and in the red glare of the dawning sun Doc Kunkel appeared, clad only in a pair of pants and carpet slippers. He was accompanied by the deputized guard who carried his black instrument bag. The crowd moved aside as the doctor squatted down by Thurlow Bunce and took a stethoscope from his medical kit. Kunkel hooked the instrument in his ears and listened briefly for the killer's breathing. Finally he looked up at Deputy Winters.

"You called me a mite too late," he reported impersonally. "This gent is *de*-ceased."

Jessie bowed her head, and said in a sort of impromptu eulogy, "Thurlow Bunce was a smart man, all right. He knew the area, and freighting, and locksmithing, and many other things. Engineering, for instance, as shown by his pumping water to his home. If he'd stayed straight, he might've amounted to something.

183

But deep down he feared and hated everybody, and he ended up the way people like that usually do. May God show him more mercy than Bunce showed his victims."

Watch for

LONE STAR AND THE TRAIL OF BLOOD

141st novel in the exciting LONE STAR series
from Jove

Coming in May!

A special offer for people who enjoy
reading the best Westerns published today.

WESTERNS!

NO OBLIGATION

Mail the coupon below

To start your subscription and receive 2 FREE WESTERNS, fill out the coupon below and mail it today. We'll send your first shipment which includes 2 FREE BOOKS as soon as we receive it.

Mail To: **True Value Home Subscription Services, Inc. P.O. Box 5235**
120 Brighton Road, Clifton, New Jersey 07015-5235

YES! I want to start reviewing the very best Westerns being published today. Send me my first shipment of 6 Westerns for me to preview FREE for 10 days. If I decide to keep them, I'll pay for just 4 of the books at the low subscriber price of $2.75 each: a total $11.00 (a $21.00 value). Then each month I'll receive the 6 newest and best Westerns to preview Free for 10 days. If I'm not satisfied I may return them within 10 days and owe nothing. Otherwise I'll be billed at the special low subscriber rate of $2.75 each: a total of $16.50 (at least a $21.00 value) and save $4.50 off the publishers price. There are never any shipping, handling or other hidden charges. I understand I am under no obligation to purchase any number of books and I can cancel my subscription at any time, no questions asked. In any case the 2 FREE books are mine to keep.

Name _____

Street Address _____ Apt. No. _____

City _____ State _____ Zip Code _____

Telephone _____

Signature _____
(if under 18 parent or guardian must sign)

Terms and prices subject to change. Orders subject
to acceptance by True Value Home Subscription
Services. Inc.

11357-3